"I'm going to require your presence all weekend...."

Luke's voice was husky with desire as he gazed at her prone nubile body.

"What do you mean? What for?" Jean shivered as he approached and slipped his hand along the length of her leg. A warm feeling engulfed her, leaving her breathless.

"Isn't it obvious? I need time to get to know you." He leaned down and kissed the inside of her ankle, then began to explore the inner flesh of her long legs with his tongue, slowly moving higher. "Days," he murmured, tickling her skin with his warm breath. "Weeks, maybe years." He nibbled sensuously on her inner thigh. "I told you—" he looked up suddenly "—I intend to take over your life!"

Dear Reader,

We at Harlequin are extremely proud to introduce our new series, **HARLEQUIN TEMPTATION**. Romance publishing today is exciting, expanding and innovative. We have responded to the ever-changing demands of you, the reader, by creating this new, more sensuous series. Between the covers of each **HARLEQUIN TEMPTATION** you will find an irresistible story to stimulate your imagination and warm your heart.

Styles in romance change, and these highly sensuous stories may not be to every reader's taste. But Harlequin continues its commitment to satisfy all your romance-reading needs with books of the highest quality. Our sincerest wish is that **HARLEQUIN TEMPTATION** will bring you many hours of pleasurable reading.

THE EDITORS

U.S.
HARLEQUIN TEMPTATION
2504 WEST SOUTHERN AVE.
TEMPE, ARIZONA
85282

CAN.
HARLEQUIN TEMPTATION
P.O. BOX 2800
POSTAL STATION "A"
WILLOWDALE, ONTARIO
M2N 5T5

Everlasting

HELEN CONRAD

Harlequin Books

TORONTO • NEW YORK • LONDON
AMSTERDAM • PARIS • SYDNEY • HAMBURG
STOCKHOLM • ATHENS • TOKYO • MILAN

To Jean Conrad, my third sister,
and a champion in her own right.

———————◆———————

Published March 1984

ISBN 0-373-25103-3

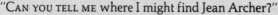

1

"CAN YOU TELL ME where I might find Jean Archer?"

Jean stiffened as she heard the deep masculine voice asking for her. She was sitting at the back of the main office in the university's Department of Sports Medicine. A tall plywood partition hid her from the view of the people entering to ask for information at the counter.

She'd been called in to fill out insurance forms, and she'd paid no attention to the comings and goings at the front of the office. But when she heard her own name, she stopped to listen.

She didn't recognize the man's voice. It had a calm assurance and a tone of authority that made her just a little wary.

"May I ask what business you have with her?"

The answering voice was that of Bette Random, the department receptionist and a good friend of Jean's. Knowing Jean as she did, Bette would understand that with a diving exhibition to perform in less than an hour, Jean was in no mood for chatting with strangers.

Jean smiled, relieved. *Bette, you're a peach,* she thought contentedly. *Now just don't let on that I'm back here and we're home free.*

"My name is Luke Chisholm. I represent Chisholm Industries. I'd like to talk to Miss Archer about a business proposition."

Jean stretched her long athletic body back in the metal

chair and sighed Endorsements, no doubt. She'd been approached by everyone from sportswear manufacturers to sports-car dealers over the last few years, but she had to be very careful of the type of deal she accepted. The hint of a profit motive on her part would destroy her amateur standing in the diving world, and that would be the end of her career as a champion diver.

No. She smiled to herself again and tilted her chin in soft pride. Not a champion diver—*the* champion diver—women's springboard and platform. The best in the country, the best in the world.

That distinction was important to her. The driving ambition that powered her rise to the top still burned in her, making her train for hours every day to make sure she stayed there. She'd been champion for seven of her twenty-eight years and by now the championship was part of her sense of identity. She'd never excelled at studies. She'd never been noted as a beauty. But she sure could dive.

Bette was standing at the end of the partition so that she could see both the man at the counter and Jean sitting at the back table, but neither could see each other.

"Do you know where Miss Archer is?" Bette asked Jean casually, glancing back to give her the opportunity to speak up if she wanted to without giving away her identity.

Jean shook her head in an emphatic no, her thick honey-brown hair, streaked liberally with sun-bleached highlights, swinging around her shoulders. Bette turned back to the man. "Sorry. I can't tell you where to find her right now. But she's diving in the exhibition at the university pool this afternoon. Perhaps you can catch her there."

Jean gritted her teeth. *Oh, Bette,* she thought. *Why didn't you tell him I'd left town on an extended tour of the Middle East?* Advertising agents were not her favorite people. Every one she'd dealt with invariably thought he had the answers to all her problems and could set her on the road to riches if she would only follow his astute advice.

"Just endorse our product, honey," was the inevitable claim, "and your name will be a household word. You'll be able to command thousands of dollars for personal appearances. Bob Hope will want you for his Christmas special. Why, you'll never have to dive again!"

That was just it. If she tried to trade her championship for personal gain she would be considered a professional and wouldn't be allowed to dive again. Not in the competitions that counted. And diving was her life.

"I'll most certainly do that," the man was answering, and Jean frowned at the suggestion of a smile in his voice. "You just tell her I'll see her a bit later."

Jean had to admit there was something in the soft southwestern drawl the man had that was warm and attractive. He sounded tall and sure of himself. She shook her head. What could you tell from a voice? He was probably short, bald and paunchy. Not that it mattered either way.

Bette came bustling back as the man left by the office door. "He knew," she exclaimed tragically.

Jean looked up in surprise. "That man who was asking for me? What did he know?"

Bette stood before her, her small pudgy hands on her generous hips, her short cap of brown curls bouncing around her round face. "He knew you were back here. Didn't you hear what he said? 'You just tell her I'll see her a bit later.' He was nodding toward where you're sitting when he said it with the most knowing smile on his face!"

Jean laughed, pulling her long, sweat-suit clad legs up

onto the seat of the chair. "He couldn't have known. If anything, it was a wild guess."

Bette shook her head. "Maybe. But he sure made me feel like a fool to get caught in that sort of trick."

Jean smiled at Bette, enjoying the emotional response she brought to every situation. The two of them had been friends since Jean had started at the University of Las Vegas six years before, using the school's exceptional diving program as a base for her training and slowly working on a degree in physical therapy, as well.

"You did me a favor by putting him off," she reassured Bette. "I couldn't talk to him just before diving."

Bette nodded. "I know that." She made an impatient movement toward the papers spread out in front of Jean. "Will you get those insurance forms filled out so I can get to work on them? You've got that meet in less than an hour."

"I know." Jean applied herself to signing the marked passages in the forms. Bette was becoming a bear about insurance forms. Her son, Andy, had been badly hurt in a riding accident and her insurance hadn't covered much of the extensive care he'd needed. Now she was determined that wouldn't happen to anyone else if she could help it.

The university swim meet was between two local teams and there was no diving competition, but Jean was making a series of exhibition dives. She would need some time for mental preparation, as she always did. Smiling, she handed Bette her pen and the stack of papers.

"Here. Have fun with these." She stood and started for the door. "And Bette . . . thanks for covering for me."

Bette nodded slowly, her bright black eyes shining as though she'd had a sudden prophecy. "I only covered for you temporarily. That man isn't going to be easy to shake off."

"Who, the Luke Chisholm character?" She shrugged. "I've had a lot of practice at getting rid of these people. Don't worry about me."

Bette's skeptical look amused her as Jean hurried out of the office and walked quickly across the grass toward the swimming stadium. There was no reason for her friend to worry. She wasn't about to waste any time listening to Luke Chisholm's sales talk. She had exactly the life she wanted right now, a life full of training and studying for a degree in physical therapy. She had no interest in the fancy cars and fur coats these advertising people were always dangling before her. The salesmen could keep their money.

When she entered the locker room it was echoing with the happy noise of swimmers preparing to challenge one another in the blue water of the pool. She smiled vaguely at one or two of them, but her mind-set was already coming into place as she pulled off her warm-up clothes and put on her burgundy-and-silver swimsuit. Stuffing her belongings, except for one small alarm clock, into a locker, she retreated to the back of the room and sat on a mat she'd prepared for herself. She set the clock for twenty minutes, then folded her legs into the lotus position, the soles of her feet up. Her hands settled gently on her knees with thumbs and forefingers forming circles, and she began to hum her mantra under her breath.

For just a moment before she'd achieved the inner peace she sought, the Chisholm person's voice crept into her mind again, and she frowned, willing it away. There was something in the sound of it that touched a responsive chord in her. All the more reason to resist it.

She concentrated on her mantra and soon the disturbingly masculine voice receded from her mind. Slowly she found the serenity she was working toward.

It worked every time. Forty-five minutes later, out on the end of the three-meter board, she had a sense of peace that allowed complete concentration. As a result, her form was superb.

Her body cut the air like a flash of silver soaring in a graceful arc, then parted the water with hardly a ripple. The applause from the stands came in waves, buoying her. This was what she lived for.

Her serenity of purpose hung on through her performance, but it finally evaporated when she saw the gaggle of reporters waiting to ambush her on the way back to the locker room.

Eleanor Sands, her diving coach, usually ran interference for her with the press, but today Eleanor was out of town and the reporters had a free rein. They stood shoulder to shoulder, watching her approach with a determined air that reminded Jean of a school of hungry barracuda.

She groaned. Of all the times for their special brand of torture. This wasn't even a real diving meet. Why didn't they take their traveling circus to surround one of the young stars of the day? What interest could they possibly have in the "old lady of diving," as she'd been called more than once by some of them.

"Hello, press people," she said brightly as she neared them. "Do I need a secret password to get into the locker room?"

"Just a little reaction if you please, Jean." Milton Fenn, veteran sportswriter for the *Nevada Star*, pushed his microphone in front of her mouth. "What do you think about the fact that Danni Worth is in town?"

Jean tried very hard not to show her real reaction. The question hit her like a punch in the stomach, knocking to life fears she wished she could keep at bay. Danni was a promising young diver who'd given her a lot of competition in the last few meets. Jean hadn't known Danni was coming to Las Vegas.

"I wish her luck at the tables," she answered lightly, hiding her real response.

"But Jean," Milton said with quick malice, "you know Danni is only seventeen. She's too young to gamble."

Then what is she here for, Jean wondered, the sinking feeling flooding her stomach. The reporter had only meant to point out the difference in the ages of the two divers, and she knew it. Members of the press were doing that more and more often lately. She didn't need to be reminded. She faced it every morning in the mirror.

"The talk is she's come to size you up as her chief obstacle to winning at the World Games here in July," another reporter said proddingly. "What's your comment?"

"Comment? Why should I comment?" She had to get out of this without losing her temper or showing her fear. "Look, Danni goes where she wants, I go where I want. We don't always have ulterior motives for every little jaunt we take."

"Miss Archer, don't you think it's time to concede that your day is over?"

The voice was unfamiliar to Jean, and as she turned to see who it was, she winced at the bright light from the television minicam.

"Aren't you getting a little old for all this? You know you've been accused of using your experience with the judges to keep your championship. Don't you think it's time to share some of the glory with the younger kids? Why don't you retire?"

Ordinarily Jean had no trouble dealing with prickly questions, but never before had anyone dared put the issue in quite such terms. She felt surrounded and very much alone. For the moment she was speechless, staring at the impassive eye of the camera, slow to defend herself but aware that this tape would undoubtedly be seen by thousands of people on the evening news.

Just as she was finally pulling her thoughts together for a response, she heard a more familiar voice supplying her answer for her.

"There's not a woman in diving who wants Jean Archer to retire."

She peered beyond the lights of the minicam to see the tall man who was speaking. She recognized the voice of Luke Chisholm, the man who'd been asking for her in the office.

"If you think any different," he was saying, "you don't understand the competitive drive of these kids. The next champion won't really feel she deserves the title unless she beats Jean to get it."

The man was anything but short and paunchy. He was nearly six feet three, with a broad chest and shoulders. He looked to be in his late thirties, though there was a sparkle to his gaze that gave him a sense of youthful energy. His hair was the color and texture of an Irish setter's coat, and his eyes gleamed with startling blue intelligence.

Those eyes swept across her now and suddenly Jean was body conscious in a way she hadn't been for years. She was used to standing in front of crowds in nothing but a wet bit of lycra cloth that left little to the imagination. Her body and its build was what diving was all about, and she knew how to present it to advantage. But something in this man's gaze told her that he wasn't looking at her as a diver. He was looking at her as a woman, and the thought sent a chill down her spine.

Suddenly she was aware of how straggly her wet hair

was, pulled back and dripping between her shoulder blades, of how her small breasts pushed against the thin stretched cloth of her suit, the nipples taut and high in the dampness. She wanted to cover herself with the towel she carried loosely in her hands, to avert her eyes and walk quickly, head down, to the protection of the locker room.

But running wasn't her style. She looked into the blue eyes and knew that everyone present thought she should be grateful for the way he'd jumped to her defense. Well, they could think again. She didn't need a protector. Especially one who was only trying to score points to get on her good side before presenting his irresistible "deal" to her.

"Diving is my life," she said evenly, ignoring what the Chisholm person had said. "Right now, I'm still competitive. I'll retire when I can't cut it anymore and not before."

She began walking purposefully toward the doors of the locker room, her eyes glinting with determination, and the reporters automatically made a path to let her through. Only one person had the nerve to try and stop her.

"Miss Archer...." Luke Chisholm actually put a hand on her arm. She stared down at it as though it were a hairy insect. "I'd like to talk to you, Miss Archer. I've got something I want to discuss with you. If you could give me a time and place...."

Salesmen were always pushy and advertising salesmen were the worst of all. If only she could convince this one to leave her alone. The questions about Danni Worth had stung, raising doubts that had bothered her lately. Was she getting too old? Could she still take it? She wanted time to mull these questions over, to get back her confidence. And this man with the penetrating-

ly blue eyes that seemed to see too deeply and the disturbingly warm voice would only add to her confusion
at this point. She had to resist him.

Impatiently she pulled away from him, risking only
one brief glance into his stunning blue eyes. "What do
you need to talk for?" she asked. "It sounded to me like
you've already got all the answers."

Jean walked proudly into the steamy locker room, relief stirring as she heard the double doors swing shut
behind her. He would wait outside those doors to
waylay her again, she was sure. But he'd be disappointed. She knew a side exit that opened directly onto
the lot where her car was parked and she would make
use of it.

Stripping off her suit, she took a quick shower and
toweled down before stepping into a lemon-yellow
terry-cloth jump suit that covered her from neck to
ankles. For some reason she stopped and used the wall
dryer on her hair instead of running a comb through its
thickness and leaving the rest to the dry desert wind as
she usually did. She stared at herself in the mirror as she
tossed her hair beneath the hot air from the machine.
The gray eyes were level but unspectacular. The nose
was straight, the cheekbones high, the mouth generous
but unremarkable. A face that blurred into the crowd.
A face to forget.

Not a touch of makeup had come near it since one dis-
astrous night in high school when her best friend,
Sharon, tried to make her beautiful for the homecoming
dance. Bowing to Sharon's superior knowledge—she
was, after all, going with a college boy at the time—Jean
allowed her friend to paint her face with blusher and
exaggerated eye shadow. Against her better judgment,
she'd gone to the dance that way. The hoots and jeers of
her fellow swim-team members cut her to the quick and

she retreated to the girls' rest room to scrub every trace of the paint from her face.

She'd never tried that again. There was no need. She'd known from the first that her looks would never get her by. She counted on her diving.

Hair dry, she pulled it back with a stretch band, collected her belongings and made her way through the chattering women in various stages of undress, until she found the fire exit. A quick shoulder to the bar and she was outside in the Nevada sunshine.

Her car was an ancient Mustang of eggshell-blue where the paint still clung. As she craned her neck, searching it out among the hundreds of other cars in the lot, she heard the sound of cowboy boots against the blacktop behind her.

"Miss Archer." the drawl was slow and unmistakable. "You didn't really think you were going to elude me that easily, did you?"

She whirled and stared at the tall man she'd thought she'd outsmarted. Out in the sunlight he seemed even taller and broader than he had before. He wore slim-fitting brushed-denim jeans and a matching jacket over a crisp white shirt, which emphasized the dark wind-whipped tan of his face and neck. He looked like a successful rancher.

His face was strong but relaxed, with a casual confidence that put her on guard. He had an easy way with women. She could see that clearly. But she'd never been at the center of much male attention and she didn't expect it. Surely that gave her an edge.

She frowned, annoyed with herself. Here she was mentally arming herself against him, as though he was a dangerous foe she had to defeat. Granted, the man disturbed her in a deeply sensual way she was unused to. But that was merely a trick he played with his know-

ing eyes and deep husky voice. She should be able to
deal with him easily.

"I don't care what you're selling," she said sharply,
backing away. "I'm not buying."

His grin was wide and infuriating. "You haven't even
had a look at my sales pitch yet."

"I know it only too well," she answered. A large car
was blocking her way, forcing her to stop her backing,
but Luke Chisholm was still coming toward her, and she
put up her hands as though to fend him off. "You're all
alike, all you sales clones. I could probably recite the
pitch in my sleep."

He came very close, but he stopped just short of her,
in a spot exactly calculated to make her upraised hands
seem ridiculous. She lowered them quickly, glaring at
him.

"In your sleep? Come on now. You don't have the
slightest idea of what I want to talk to you about." His
blue eyes were laughing at her. She couldn't stay around
for this.

She managed to slip along the car until she was free of
his entrapment, and she started walking down the
length of the lot, searching hurriedly for a sign of her
car.

"Well?" he prompted, walking right beside her, his
long stride mocking her quick steps.

Where was her car? She stopped at the end of the lot,
unable for the life of her to remember where she'd
parked. The Chisholm person stopped with her and she
flashed him a quick look.

"All right, Mr. Salesman," she began, but he stopped
her with a modest smile.

"Uh—owner of the company," he corrected.

She shrugged. "They're the worst kind." She let her
gray eyes examine him with more arrogance than she

was feeling. "What do you make at your company? Swimsuits? Do you want me to put one on and smile for the camera, stretching out to show it off?"

He cocked a thick bronze eyebrow. "Sounds pretty good—" he began, but she cut him off.

"Or maybe you make cereal. You want me to put a spoonful of the disgusting stuff in my mouth and force a toothy grin." She struck a dramatic pose. " 'This delicious cereal, full of crunchy nuggets, made me into the champion I am today.' "

She challenged him with a stabbing stare. "Do you make cereal?"

He shook his head, eyes dancing. "No, Miss Archer. I don't make cereal."

"Okay." She was warming to this game now, though she started off looking for her car again. He followed along, seemingly ready to hear her whole routine. "Maybe it's crackers. Or chicken soup. For some reason, the fact that I hold a can of it in my hand and smile is supposed to convince thousands that they can be diving stars too, if they only buy it and eat it. It's ridiculous."

"I agree."

"And even if you sell swimming pools or make bathing caps, who cares if I like them? What difference does it make?"

"You got me there."

She stopped and turned to face him. "Just what do you make?"

"Footballs."

Her jaw dropped, but she quickly recovered. "Footballs?"

He nodded. "Miss Archer, my name is Luke Chisholm. I run Chisholm Industries." He stuck out his hand and she took it a bit numbly. "And I have a business proposition to make to you."

"Footballs?" she asked again.

"Well, that's what we manufacture. Actually, we're into other things as well—"

"Oh, no." She backed away, shaking her head, then began walking briskly between cars again. "It's life insurance, isn't it? I don't want life insurance. I don't need life insurance. I don't want to leave anyone happy when I die."

Her car had to be somewhere in this infuriating lot. If only she could take a minute to concentrate on the search without this giant following her every move.

"Miss Archer, I assure you, I won't try to sell you any life insurance."

Another dead end. She stopped at the corner of the lot and looked back over the gleaming car tops baking in the desert sun.

"Footballs, huh?" She gazed at him speculatively, responding against her will to the warmth of his personality. "Maybe you want me to hold the football with my finger while some hulking jock kicks it out of my hand?" She shook her head slowly, finding it difficult to release his sparkling blue gaze once she'd been caught in it. "No, probably not. I'm not quite the type for that, am I?"

She tried to push past him, but he stopped her with a hand on her shoulder. "Not the type for what?" he asked softly.

She shrugged, trying to pull out from under his touch. "The model type. Those girls have to be beautiful."

It was only the truth. She knew what she looked like. The fact didn't hurt like it had when she was in her teens. She'd learned to accept it. But she found it hard to keep from flinching under the puzzled scrutiny Luke was giving her after her statement.

"You are beautiful," he said at last, and she gasped at

the sheer effrontery of the lie, but he didn't let her get in
a protest. "You've got the most beautiful body I think
I've ever seen."

What, this old thing? She almost laughed aloud. She
knew her body was beautiful in the apex of a swan dive,
or at the entry when every muscle was rigid. But standing here on a man-to-woman basis? Hardly.

"That's awful nice of you, Mr. Chisholm, but not
quite in line with popular opinion. I think my body is
most often kindly referred to as 'boyishly slim.'"

"Boyish?" His laugh was loud and scornful, and she
gazed up at him in surprise. "There's nothing boyish
about you, Jean Archer." Suddenly his hands had
swooped down to circle her waist. "I never knew a boy
with hips like these," he told her huskily.

Something was happening—something that Jean
didn't like at all. Her gaze was locked into his, locked in
a way that trapped her, left her helpless. The pressure of
his hands on her waist, his fingers spanning the narrow
width of it, was as hot as molten metal, sending a
warmth rushing through her that she'd never experienced before.

Then his hands were moving up, rubbing the fuzzy
cloth between them and her body and she ached at the
dizzying sensation.

"Why do you hide your beautiful body under this
silly cover-up?" he asked softly. "At least show a bit of
skin."

He took hold of the tab to the zipper that ran from the
neckline to the crotch of her jump suit and began to pull
it down, slowly but steadily.

"Don't," she whispered, still lost in his eyes, but
struggling to regain control of herself.

"Why not?" He stopped when his fingers were between her breasts and the two sides of the opening

peeled back to reveal an attractive cleavage. His gaze surveyed his handiwork with approval. "That looks so much more inviting."

Freed from the spell of his eyes, she found her sharp tongue once again. "But invitations are not open to the public, Mr. Chisholm," she snapped. "So I'll thank you to consider yourself off the guest list as of now."

She tried to pull away from him, but he wouldn't let her go.

"Wait a minute, Jean," he coaxed. "We haven't even begun to talk about what I came to discuss."

"Send me a letter," she suggested, slipping out of his grasp, and suddenly there was her car only steps away.

"Jean. . . ." He tried to take her arm again, but she spun, pushing back from him and darting toward her car. She was sure he would follow her, but she planned to make any sort of chase out of the parking lot just about impossible.

2

JEAN HAD EXPECTED HIM to follow her, and when she found time to unlock her door and throw in her things without Luke Chisholm breathing down her neck, she turned to see what had happened to him. To her surprise, she saw him down on one knee, the other leg stretched out straight in front of him, as though he'd fallen and was having difficulty getting up.

She hesitated. Here was her chance to get away. But what if he was really hurt? After all, with her training in physical therapy, could she just drive off and leave him?

"What's the matter?" she called, but he only shook his head, not looking up. *He's in pain,* she thought, and without another qualm she ran back to see what had happened.

"What is it?" she asked anxiously, kneeling down beside him. "What's the matter?"

He raised his head to look at her as though reluctant to meet her eyes. "It's nothing. Trick knee. Don't give it another thought." A grimace lined his face, then was gone, and he smiled a bit wanly. "I'll have to catch up with you another time."

Jean sat back on her heels and looked at him. He was trying to act as though this was nothing much, but she'd worked with all kinds of disabilities and she knew pain when she saw it. The white line around his mouth told her all she needed to know.

"What happened? Did you trip? Did you land on the knee?"

His chuckle sounded forced. "No, I did not trip. I just got walloped by that mean right hook you carry around with you, girl. You got that thing registered with the police?"

She started to speak, then closed her mouth again. She'd lashed out at him as she whirled away, but surely she hadn't hit him hard enough for this.

He read the skepticism in her eyes. "Well, you didn't exactly knock me off my feet, but you did throw me off-balance and my knee went out at the same time." He winced and reached forward to rub the area above the joint. "Don't give it another thought. Happens all the time."

"I really did it?" she asked, full of remorse. "I'm sorry. I never dreamed. . . . What can I do to help you?"

Slowly and painfully he pulled himself up to lean against a nearby car. "Not a thing. Just let me get through it my own way."

That was, of course, impossible. She couldn't leave him here writhing in pain. "I'm going to call for the campus doctor," she told him crisply. "You just stay right here."

"I'm not likely to get too far on this leg." His tone was ironic, but he smiled at her. "Don't bother calling any doctors. That's not what I need right now."

This was certainly no time to play macho man. She frowned sternly. "Don't be ridiculous. That's exactly what you need."

"No." He reached out and took her hand as though to stop her. "I've been to doctors before. All they want to do is shoot you full of stuff that makes your head go fuzzy. I don't want that."

His hand felt warm as it curled around her fingers.

She found herself holding it as though to communicate her compassion through touch. He looked so helpless, like a wounded stag. Much as she'd resented his masculinity before when he'd been well, she hated seeing him weakened this way.

"At least let me take you to the clinic."

He shook his head, his smile bittersweet in a way that tore at her. "No, just leave me here," he said sadly. "It might go away in half an hour or so."

She stared at him. "What if it doesn't?"

He shrugged. "Oh, I guess I'll just wait until it does. It's never cramped up for more than twenty-four hours before."

She tightened her grip on his hand. "Let me help you over to the grass."

"No, no." He shook his head. "You just go on about your business. I'll be okay." He shifted his weight as though trying to maneuver into a more comfortable position.

"I can't just leave you here in the middle of the parking lot."

Of course she couldn't. Reluctantly she began to face what she must do. After all, this was what she was trained for. She was being presented with a ready-made opportunity to put all that experience, all those hours of classroom lectures in physical therapy into action.

"Come on." She tugged on his arm. "Let me pull you up. You can lean on me and we'll make it over to my car just fine."

"Your car? I told you, I won't go to any clinic."

"I'm not taking you to a clinic," she said evenly, refusing to meet his eyes. "I'm taking you to my apartment where I can work on that knee."

Was it her imagination, or had something new entered his voice when he spoke again?

"Just exactly what do you mean, 'work on my knee'?"

"I'm taking courses in physical therapy here at the university," she told him. "I've had a lot of experience with trick knees. Maybe I can do something to help you."

"I wouldn't want to get in the way," he said smoothly, but he was already pulling up to lean on her. "I don't want to be a burden."

"Don't worry," she answered, struggling to bring enough of his weight into proper balance. "Consider yourself practice material. I want to get good at this before finals."

Getting him into the car was not easy. He was so very tall. At one point, she almost suggested he lie on top of the car so she could tie him flat and carry him home like a load of lumber, but she didn't think he would take kindly to the idea.

Finally he was situated in the front seat with both legs stretched out straight in front of him, and she was able to go around to the driver's seat and start the car.

Neither of them spoke much as she directed her Mustang along the campus drive and then out into the community. She glanced over at him once. He was staring ahead and tiny beads of sweat shimmered on his upper lip. She felt a sickening surge of sympathy for him, then returned her attention to the road.

Her apartment was in a small building close to the campus. Luckily it was on the first floor with an entrance on the street. Jean parked in front and left the car to unlock her door before coming back to start unfolding Luke.

"Take it slow," she urged as he vaulted out of the seat. "You don't want to damage the tendon if it's under stress."

There it was again, the flash of something in those

blue eyes. What was it? Humor? Triumph? She stopped and stared at him suspiciously, but when he turned to look at her again his eyes were guileless.

"Put all your weight on me," she encouraged, then staggered under the load.

"Sure you can take it?" he asked, and this time she was certain of the humor in his voice. But she was much too busy maneuvering him into her living room and down onto the couch to pay any attention.

Her apartment was small but adequate for her needs. Large windows let sunlight flow in unencumbered and she took advantage of that with an abundance of plants of every description. Each flat surface was covered with a clay or ceramic pot, spilling over with greenery.

The furnishings were simple. A small round wooden table was bracketed by two wicker chairs, and her beige chintz couch faced an armchair and a low Danish modern coffee table covered with diving magazines and potted geraniums.

She helped Luke settle on the couch with his legs stretched out before him.

"Your pants are too tight," she said impatiently as she gazed down at him.

His eyes widened. "Sorry."

She could see the corners of his mouth threatening to turn up and she quickly explained herself. "I don't think you'll be able to roll the pant leg high enough above your knee to do us any good."

He nodded. "You're probably right."

"So you're going to have to take off your pants," she told him dispassionately.

"Am I now?" His grin was wide and interested.

"Of course. How else am I going to get at your knee?"

"How else?" he echoed, reaching in front to unbuckle his belt. "What could be simpler?"

She avoided looking into his sparkling eyes, sure that he would be enjoying this to the hilt. She was a professional and she would treat him in a professional manner. There was no problem as long as she kept her head.

But keeping her head might prove more difficult than she'd at first supposed. She'd noticed a strange involuntary reaction to this man on a sensual level from the start. It wasn't like her to tingle at a man's touch, to feel a slight flush spread across her cheeks at meeting his glance. What was it about this man that was different from all the others she'd known throughout her life?

He was handsome—absolutely. His blue eyes radiated a bright humor that seemed to mock her attempt to keep him at a distance. He was powerfully built, but she was used to that. Most swimmers were, too, and male divers were notoriously well muscled.

What was there about him that seemed to catch her off-balance every time?

She glanced at him struggling out of his slacks and knew she could either stay to help him undress or leave the room. There was really very little choice in the matter.

"I'll get my equipment," she mumbled as she fled down the hall and into her bedroom. Whirling around the corner, she stopped. She held onto her door and stared into her full-length mirror on the opposite wall.

Was she crazy? Here she was with a strange man taking his pants off in her living room. Nothing like this had ever happened to her before. A slow tentative grin crept over her face. It certainly was exciting.

He'd said she was beautiful. Her grin broadened as she looked at herself in the glass. He was lying, but what a nice lie. No one had ever said that to her before. Not that she'd given many men the chance.

Dating required time and effort she just never had.

The few times she had become involved with a man, it had usually ended in unhappiness all around.

She recalled Keith, the love of her life when she was nineteen. He'd been a diver too, but when he failed time after time in national competitions to make the sort of name for himself that Jean had, his resentment grew bigger and bigger until it finally overwhelmed their relationship.

That was when she vowed to stay away from divers. The next man she got involved with was a local contractor. He had no connection with diving whatsoever. The trouble was, he was so far removed from the sport he couldn't understand why she had to spend so much time at it, why she wasn't available when he needed a companion, why she had to travel so much. He'd soon looked around for a woman who was more readily available.

For a long time she'd sworn off dating altogether. Then Jeffrey Marks came into her life.

Jeffrey! She glanced quickly at her watch. She'd forgotten all about him. He was due to arrive in less than an hour.

Good old Jeffrey. Jean supposed she would marry him someday. They'd been going together for almost two years now and their friends expected it, though the two of them had never discussed it in so many words.

Actually, there'd been a time more than a year ago, when Jeffrey had seemed ready to talk about it. But there'd been a big meet in the offing and Jean had brushed aside his attempts to get serious. She didn't have time for that. She had to concentrate on her training.

"Serious" was a state alien to Jeffrey's constitution, anyway. He had a wisecrack to fit any occasion and when the two of them were together they sometimes acted like a pair of high-school kids.

Jeffrey was good fun, and she hadn't really ever had time for more than that. Ever since she'd become a diver, the training had come first and everything else came when diving was over. She'd had quite a job wedging in enough courses in physical therapy to bring her to the brink of her degree, much less adding a close relationship to the schedule.

Jeffrey had been participating in the physical therapy program as a resident at the local hospital when she first met him. He'd taught the introductory courses in physiology, and the first time his eyes had met hers, staring earnestly as he lectured, he'd grinned and she'd smiled back. There'd been a spark of humor between them right from the first.

Now Jeffrey had his own private practice. They'd toyed with the idea of adding her as his in-office therapist when she'd completed work on her degree, but nothing definite had been decided.

"I'm ready."

Her heart lurched at the sound of Luke Chisholm's voice coming from the living room. *Steady*, she told herself. *Complete calm is essential.*

"Just a minute," she answered, digging wildly through the stack of books and papers overflowing from her bookcase in the corner of her room. She finally found her notes covering knee injuries. She was fairly sure of what she was doing, but it never hurt to look over a few reminders. "I'll be right out."

After reading quickly, she rummaged in her closet and pulled out a boxed ultrasound instrument and other assorted implements before returning to the living room. "Here we are," she said a bit breathlessly, refusing to look at the man on the couch and busying herself with opening the cases of her instruments instead. Her gaze fell on the neat pile his slacks made on the coffee table, but she looked away. "I'll make a few tests first."

"My examination?"

"Oh, no," she said quickly, looking into his blue eyes and then away again. "Only doctors give examinations. And only a trained physician can fully prescribe treatment. What therapists do is called evaluation or assessment."

"But it means the same thing." His voice was warm with humor.

"Yes," she admitted reluctantly, "just about."

She closed one case and opened another. The time had arrived when she would have to turn and begin testing his knee, but somehow she couldn't force herself to do it. Her breath was coming faster and she knew panic was setting in. She would have to grit her teeth and turn or he would know how scared she was.

"All right, I guess I have everything," she said brightly, steeling herself. "Let's see the knee."

She helped him extend both legs down the length of the couch, then she sat down beside him, making sure her gaze took in nothing but the leg displayed before her. But what she saw made her gasp and look immediately into his eyes.

"What have you done to this thing?" she demanded, outraged at the condition she'd found it in. Long pale scars lined either side of the knee and two bright red crescents circled the kneecap like angry wounds.

"Just a little cut and paste." His smile was lopsided. "I've had a few knee operations."

"A few! This looks like it was used for target practice by a whole class of budding orthopedic surgeons." She frowned down at the tortured leg. "What was the problem?"

He sighed and leaned back. "Football."

She gazed into his face again. her eyebrows high with surprise. "Making footballs ruins knees?"

"Not exactly. But playing football sure does its share."

"Oh."

She was going to have to touch him. The skin of his leg was golden brown and the reddish brown hair curled crisply along his muscled thigh. She found herself holding her breath as she reached out to touch the area around his knee.

The hair was rough and it tickled her palm. The skin was warm. He was just a man. Nothing else. She let out her breath and began to probe with gentle firmness for evidence of injury as she would with any other patient.

She was sitting forward on the couch with her back to his body, leaning over the stretched out leg. "What kind of football do you play to do this kind of damage?" she asked, as much to fill the awkward silence as to find the answer.

"I don't play anymore. But I spent a good many years at it." The smile was back in his voice. "Are you going to tell me you've never heard of Luke Chisholm, defensive back for the San Francisco 49ers?"

She shook her head, her fingers sliding along the tendon, judging the condition of the muscles that surrounded the knee joint. "I've never been much of a fan," she said abstractedly. "Were you good?"

"Was I good?" he echoed, his voice a low rumble. "Darling, I was the best."

She flashed him a look back over her shoulder. "What did you do with this leg—use it as a club?"

"I used it as a launcher a few too many times. Got hit when I wasn't prepared a few too many times." She could feel his shrug. "The hazards of the game."

She turned in her seat feeling fully professional. "Tell me about the operations. What was the diagnosis? What were the treatments?"

His frown told her he didn't find this a pleasant topic. "The last they told me was that I've lost most of the cartilage that protects the joint from the kneecap. That hurts a bit. And the tendon is weakened on one side. It sometimes catches and locks as it did in the parking lot this afternoon."

"When was the last time you had this x-rayed?"

He shook her question away with a toss of his head. "Keep on rubbing it that way. It feels better every minute you touch it."

She resumed the light massage, using small circular motions with the fingertips of both hands to stimulate the circulation and relax the muscles. A feeling of carefree relief was coursing through her. She felt almost light-headed. This was easy. She was doing her job in a professional manner despite her lack of experience and despite the disturbing qualities of the man under her hands.

"You really must see a doctor," she told him sternly, not looking back to see how he took her statement. "I can't begin to know for sure what your trouble is. I can only give you some temporary relief from the stiffness and pain."

"You make me feel much better than any doctor ever did." His voice was low and husky, and suddenly she felt his warm hand at the back of her neck.

She froze, not really sure of what he was doing, and he began to caress the top of her spine as gently as she was massaging his knee.

"You'll have to let me pay you back in kind," he told her softly.

His hand was so large she almost felt he might snatch

her up with it and hold her in the air. She closed her eyes for just a moment, allowing herself the pleasure of his touch.

Unprofessional, she told herself sternly. *Totally unprofessional.* She slipped out from under his hand and left the couch to retrieve the piece of equipment she had waiting.

"This is an ultrasound device," she said stiffly, talking too fast but unable to stop herself. "It generates sound waves that might help your knee. The energy is transformed to heat as it travels through the tissues. . . ."

She sounded like a lecturer with a hall full of students, but she didn't care. Anything to keep from looking at the man and thinking about the reality of this awkward situation.

"I'll just rub on a little mineral oil and you'll have a real demonstration." She poured some oil onto a piece of cotton gauze and worked it briskly across his flesh. "Here we go." She plugged in the sound head and leaned down to place the device on his leg, not daring to sit by him again. "Can you feel the warmth?"

He didn't answer and she wondered how long she could stare down at the ultrasound head as though she really needed to watch it every second. "You should be feeling a mild tingling sort of heat. The waves can generate heat five centimeters below the surface of the skin—"

Suddenly she heard the cord being yanked from the wall socket and the device went dead in her hand. She looked up in surprise and Luke reached out to take it from her, placing it on the coffee table.

"What are you doing?" she asked, stunned. "Was it too hot? Sometimes if you don't move it quickly enough—"

"It wasn't too hot." He inched himself a bit higher

against the corner of the couch and reached out to pull her down with him. "But you're too nervous."

"Nervous!" She was at a loss for words.

He nodded solemnly. "I don't know if you're scared of me or of what you're doing, but either way you'll do better once you've calmed down."

"Scared of you!" Her eyes flashed dark fire. "Don't be ridiculous. I've faced down more formidable men than you, Luke Chisholm."

His smile was lopsided. "In a fight, I've no doubt you're victorious every time." His voice deepened imperceptibly. "But we're not fighting, are we?"

No, they weren't fighting, but the adrenaline was flowing as fiercely as though they were.

"I'm going to teach you how to get rid of that tension," he said quietly.

She stared at him. Some impulse to resist flared briefly, but this was all so new, so unexpected, she felt almost that she should wait to explore it fully before reacting.

"You're obviously a very competent physical therapist, Jean Archer," he told her, his eyes laughing. "But you'll never find success in this profession if you don't learn to relax."

"Relax?" she echoed dully. *Oh, Jean,* a part of her was crying, *where is your strength?*

He nodded solemnly. "Relax."

Sitting there, facing him, her eyes were level with his and she couldn't seem to look away from them. She stared in wonder at the warm sparkle in his gaze as he pulled her band from her hair, letting the silky waves fall over her shoulders, then took her face between his hands and drew it slowly toward him.

She was sure he was going to kiss her, but instead he stopped when he had her in comfortable range and began massaging her temples lightly with his fingers.

"You've got to get rid of the tension in yourself before you can work it out of others," he murmured, letting his hands work slowly down to circle her neck, moving softly all the time.

She couldn't answer him. She was still lost in the depths of his crystal eyes, swimming in the sultry sea he'd drawn her into. *He's hypnotizing me*, she thought dreamily. *Isn't it wonderful?*

His hands covered her shoulders, working the muscles into pliant putty. She gazed at him, noting the laugh lines that radiated from his eyes, the dark lashes that curled against his skin, the tan weather-roughened texture of his face.

"Isn't that better?" he asked softly.

His face was close to hers, just inches away. She closed her eyes, letting the warm languor he created spread through her, feeling every muscle, every bone, melt under his touch.

Why didn't he kiss her? Anticipation began to tingle in her breast, catching at her breath. When was he going to kiss her?

"Don't you feel more relaxed now?" His hands slipped up to cup her face, but he made no move to bring her in against him. Instead, his voice suddenly crisp and businesslike, he asked, "Ready to get back to work?"

Her eyes flew open, indignation sparking from their depths. He wasn't going to kiss her at all! Here she'd been so sure the interlude was just an excuse to bring it about. And all the time he'd been serious. He was only trying to get her to relax.

His blue eyes were laughing at her. He knew exactly what was going on in her mind. He thought he had a scared little ninny here, someone who knew nothing about handling men. Jean's natural temper flared. She'd show *him* just how scared she was.

"Not quite ready." she said distinctly, narrowing her eyes and reaching out to cup his face the same way he was cupping hers. "Just one more thing."

Slowly, deliberately, she pulled his face toward hers, ignoring the laughter in his eyes, concentrating on his full well-defined lips. She'd planned only a quick peck of a kiss, but once she had him, she found herself wanting more. The sensation of his warmth only increased her need, and her own lips parted to let her tongue flicker against his smooth mouth, coaxing it to open as well.

She felt the chuckle in his chest rather than heard it, and suddenly he was leaning back against the pillows again, pulling her down on top of him.

"You learn quickly, Jean Archer," he murmured against her open mouth. "I must say, I like your methods."

He didn't give her time to answer before he claimed her lips again, sliding his tongue alongside hers, exploring her hidden fire just as she longed to explore his. Her hands had found their way to his chest and were now the only thing holding their bodies apart. She could feel his flesh beneath the crisp cotton shirt. It was firm and vibrant in a way that sent a current through her hands and left them tingling with excitement. Involuntarily they began to move across his chest, searching for the opening of his shirt, longing to feel him unencumbered by the thin cloth.

His arms were around her, holding her close atop him, and his hands were working gently across her back, kneading softly into her flesh. She felt a moan rising in her throat, then heard it expressed aloud as she slipped her hands higher, letting her body mold to his, feeling the pressure of his warmth against her breasts. Her fingers combed into his thick hair, luxuriating in the wealth of it, and she moaned again.

It was time to pull away. The joke was over. But something was keeping her from doing that. She stirred from her lethargy. She had to do it. If she didn't, who would?

"Hey." She placed her palms upon his chest again and raised herself, letting her hair fall down around her face as she looked at him lying beneath her. "I think it's time to get back to work."

He didn't protest but grinned at her like a lazy cat stretching in the sun, before reaching up to stroke her cheek with one calloused finger. "Whatever you say, lady. You're the therapist."

Her cheeks were burning as she realized just what she'd done, but she wasn't sorry she'd done it. She could look him in the eye now without feeling she must look quickly away. She was no longer embarrassed by his lack of clothing. In fact, she'd relaxed, just as he'd told her to.

"You lie still," she told him sternly, "while I finish this."

She busied herself plugging in the ultrasound and placing the sound head on his knee while he lay back, his arms folded casually behind his head, and watched her, amusement softening his face. When she met his eyes she was able to smile back at him without hesitation.

"I hope this will help you," she said. "But you really must see an orthopedic surgeon. I don't know how you ever let this knee get in such horrible shape. If football was so bad for it, you shouldn't have been playing the game."

He chuckled at that. "Football was my life at that

time. I couldn't imagine not playing it. I did a lot in order to stay in the game."

She glanced at him shrewdly. "Like letting them dope up your leg and playing on it when it was numb?"

He nodded slowly, all humor gone. "That's right."

"That's pretty stupid," she charged.

His smile was cold. "Stupid, but typical. I would've done anything to win." He moved restlessly. "That's part of my nature," he continued, almost more to himself than to her. "I don't like losing. I play for keeps."

She turned off the ultrasound and put it aside. "That sounds pretty ruthless. You can't always win. Haven't you ever heard that it's the way you play the game that counts?"

He grinned. "I've heard it. I've just never believed it. When I get in a corner I use everything I can to fight my way out, no matter what."

"No matter who gets hurt?" she asked suddenly, then bit her lip. Where had that question come from?

He was looking at her as though she'd pried a little too close to the bone. "I've never willingly hurt anyone," he said defensively. "It's only my own skin I put on the line."

She couldn't leave it alone. "Ever looked behind you to see how many bodies were stacking up?" What was the matter with her? She was attacking him as though she knew something awful about his background.

He reached out to catch her by the hand, his eyes searching for the reason for her concern. "What are you afraid of, Jean?" he asked softly. "I would never hurt you."

She tried to laugh and succeeded in a fair facsimile. "You couldn't hurt me if you tried," she announced airily. "Let's give the knee a test here and see how your flexion is coming along."

She made him straighten out his leg, then try to pull it back as far as he could against his thigh.

"Not very good," she noted dourly. "I'm going to call a surgeon I know and make an appointment for you right now."

"Jean." He stood up, wincing slightly but able to stand fully on both legs. "You've done marvels for my knee. More than I deserve. But leave the appointment making to me."

She looked at him a bit anxiously. "You promise you'll go?"

He sighed. "I promise."

She frowned. "How am I going to know if you keep that promise?" She regretted it as soon as the words were out of her mouth. He would think she was angling to see him again. She turned from him quickly, trying to think of a way to alter the impression she'd just given him. "Not that I care," she amended gruffly. "Put your pants on."

He reached for them, but only to drape them across his arm while he watched her putting away her equipment. "You're going to have to give up terry-cloth jump suits," he drawled as he watched. "To hide a body like yours behind all that fuzz is a crime."

She met his eyes but couldn't work up a feeling of outrage. "Put on your pants," she reminded him.

He stood easily now, his legs wide, the pain in his knee only a memory. "You'd look best naked, I'll bet," he told her wisely. "If you have to wear something, you ought to stick to sheer material that lets every line show beneath it. Something in pastel colors that would swirl around you like a cloud." He shook his head. "The human body is a work of art, especially when it looks like yours. It ought to be on display."

She loved to hear the silliness he was talking, even

though it was meaningless. She couldn't hold back a grin as she packed away the last of her lotions and lifted her face to his. "Is that why you're resisting clothes yourself?" she asked innocently. "Are you planning an exhibition?"

He looked so attractive with his hair falling down over his forehead and his shirttail hanging down almost to his tanned legs—an eerie combination of very mature masculinity and naughty little boy.

"Not exactly." He grinned back, then suddenly he stepped closer and his hand was curling around her upper arm. She felt her pulse begin to quicken again. He carried an excitement with him that her body responded to even when she most wanted it to remain impassive. "I owe you, you know. What do you usually charge for house calls?"

She stared at his hand. The fingers were long and finely sculptured, like something Michelangelo might have created. The nails were cut straight and short. Along the wide back of his hand a few golden red hairs sprang up, looking as tough as the man himself.

She swallowed, fighting back stray thoughts. This was very odd. She never analyzed every detail of the men she knew. It was almost as though she was looking for reasons to feel something special for him, and that was a dangerous thing to do. The man was here now, but he would soon be going. And once he was gone, she wouldn't find much pleasure in remembering how much she'd been attracted to him. Much better to wipe those thoughts out from the beginning.

She gazed resolutely up into his eyes. "I don't charge for house calls when it's my house," she answered him.

Looking into his eyes had been a mistake. As his warmth wrapped around her, she couldn't look away. She felt as though she was walking slowly into a tropic

sea the color of his crystal blue gaze. The water was lapping at her ankles, then her knees. Water as soft and
sensual as velvet, water that could carry her away to
another place and coax her to do things she never would
have dreamed possible.

Then he smiled, and it was as though she'd plunged
in, the water spraying up around her as she let herself
fall, and he was kissing her again, his mouth as hot as
the sun would be above her water-cooled body in its
sparkling lagoon.

She didn't dare breathe. She was underwater, spinning like a flower caught in the current, and his heat was
filling her with life, flowing into every corner. She
burned as his arms came around her, meeting his body
with hers arched in eager anticipation of his strength.

His kiss was more masterful this time. He was no
longer surprised and amused. Now he was exploring the
potential between them, reaching with experimental interest to see what they could create together.

She closed her mind off to misgivings. She was enjoying the kiss, enjoying the thrill his masculinity sent
through her, wishing it might never end.

Their mouths met and met again, tongues joining in a
reckless dance that ignited a flame between them. His
large hands moved across her back, working with gentle
mastery over her flesh until they slid down to curl
around her bottom, pulling her in hard against him, and
she gasped at the evidence of his awakened desire.

He didn't protest as she pulled away, though he
seemed to let her go reluctantly. There was a new light
burning in his eyes and she looked down, unwilling to
meet and analyze it. She was trembling. How she
prayed he couldn't tell! But she was, and she knew he
was affecting her in ways no other man ever had before.
That knowledge excited and frightened her, and she

wished she could have a moment alone to get her bearings.

"So you don't charge for house calls," he went on softly, picking up their conversation where they'd left off. "How about office calls?"

"It's been my pleasure." She winced at the connotations he might derive from that. He stood in front of her, unmoving as a tree, and she looked up into his gaze again, trying to keep a flippant smile on her face even though she felt like screaming into a pillow.

"I can't let you get away with that," he countered. "You've got to let me pay you back somehow."

Oh, you've paid me back, she thought to herself. *You've given me things I've never had before.* But that was hardly a thing she could tell him. Instead, she shrugged and said, "Be nice to the next person you see on the street. Maybe we'll start a chain that will reach around the world."

His mouth twisted. "Fair enough. But you've also got to let me take you out to dinner."

Her eyes widened. "Out to dinner?" she echoed. That surprised her. She wasn't his type and she knew it. If she wasn't careful she might almost begin to believe he wanted to date her.

She clenched her jaw tightly. No, she mustn't start believing in fairy tales. Once she started doing that, she'd really get herself hurt.

He was nodding, eyes sparkling, unaware of her unease. "Out to dinner. You've heard of dinner? It's that big meal people tend to eat after the sun goes down."

"I know what dinner is." She started to laugh and had to avert her gaze from his. "I. . .I can't."

He put a finger beneath her chin and raised it. "You're not still scared of me, are you?"

If you only knew how much, she thought shakily. "I

never was scared of you," she retorted. She wondered if he would believe her words or the evidence he saw before him. Surely he'd noticed how her fingers were trembling, how nervously she was twisting them around the things she held in her arms. "I can't go out with you tonight. I have a date."

"Break it," he said without hesitation, and she looked at him feeling a mixture of awe and scorn. Women probably broke dates for him all the time. It meant nothing to him.

"I can't."

"Why not?"

Why not? Her mind was getting as fuzzy as her jump suit. Suddenly she knew that she wanted to go out with him very badly. "He...Jeffrey...he'll be here any minute...."

His hand slipped down to curl loosely around her neck, caressing lightly, almost absently. "Let me try to bribe you," he said smoothly. "Think of Chateaubriand for two. Shrimp scampi, their long pink tails floating in butter. Oysters on the half shell. Lobster Marrienne."

Still she shook her head, though the menu he was running through was making her mouth water. She knew Jeffrey was planning dinner at the nearest chain coffee shop where patty melt was a specialty. The menu Luke was reciting sounded like heaven compared to that.

"We still haven't discussed the business proposition I have for you."

"Oh." Suddenly all the excitement began to fade. She'd forgotten about that. No wonder he wanted to take her to dinner. He hadn't got what he came for.

But before she had time to make a sharp retort, the doorbell rang.

Panic leapt into her throat but she quelled it firmly. There was nothing to hide here—nothing to be ashamed of. And having thought that, she almost giggled, seeing Luke's half-naked state. "It's Jeffrey!" she hissed. "Will you *please* put your pants on?"

He smiled. "If I go to the door for you this way, I guarantee I'll get rid of him in thirty seconds."

"No doubt," she growled, not sure whether to laugh or cry, "but I don't want to get rid of him. Can't you understand that?"

With seeming reluctance, he began to dress while she waited impatiently, jumping when the doorbell rang again, motioning for Luke to hurry.

"Hi, Jeffrey," she said at last as she flung the door open. Her friend stood before her in a gray business suit, his light brown hair combed slickly down, his face handsome in a carefree boyish way. He stood carelessly, legs wide, shoulders hunched, hands in his pockets.

"What took you so long?" he answered, his annoyance evident.

"Sorry." Luke had come up behind her and was now smiling benignly at Jeffrey. "She had to wait until I got my pants on."

Shock froze them all for a moment. Then Jean felt a quick rush of sympathy for Jeffrey, who looked totally bewildered. "Don't listen to him," she said reassuringly, drawing Jeffrey into the apartment. Her glance at Luke threw daggers, but he winked at her and sat back down on the couch as though completely at home.

"This is Luke Chisholm. Luke, meet Dr. Jeffrey Marks." She licked her lower lip quickly, then gestured toward her instruments. "Mr. Chisholm has a traumatized knee. I've been using ultrasound on it." She looked desperately at Luke for help, but he only threw back his head and smiled, waiting.

He was enjoying this to the hilt, she realized with disbelief. What havoc he was creating in her life! "It's the truth," she said. "That's why he had his pants off." Surely Jeffrey's ever-present sense of humor would get them through this.

Jeffrey looked from Jean to Luke as though gazing at creatures from another planet. Jean moved closer to him, watching his eyes. "Come on Luke," she said carefully. "Show Jeffrey your knee."

Luke groaned, lolling back against the pillows. "I'd have to take my pants back off to do that."

Jean grinned, coaxing a smile from Jeffrey. "Exactly."

Jeffrey managed to conjure up a wavering grin and keep it plastered on his wide freckled face. "Haven't I warned you before about these door-to-door salesmen?" he said, and she knew it was going to be all right.

"I haven't found out what he's selling, yet," she replied.

Jeffrey gave her a look of mock surprise. "Oh, yeah? Taking his pants off should've given you the first clue." He added quickly, before she could respond, "Where did you find him?"

She cast a sideways look at the man on the couch. "At school. He was chasing me around the parking lot when he began to fall apart."

Jeffrey nodded wisely. "Pieces flying everywhere, no doubt. I've seen it happen before. It's this modern age. Shoddy workmanship."

Luke's laugh was low and rich and it rumbled out to encase them both, stopping the train of joking they were on, making them both turn to stare at him.

Jean noticed how he dominated the room. She and Jeffrey were ready to react to whatever he did or said to them. They were like children in the presence of someone older. She could feel the power flowing from him and knew he was a natural leader.

"Sit down, Jeffrey," Luke told her friend genially. "I'd

like to pay back Jean's kindness to me by taking her out
to dinner, but I understand the two of you already have
plans. I would appreciate it if both of you would join me
for dinner at my hotel."

Jeffrey peered at him suspiciously. "Where is it that
you're staying?" he began, then stopped, staring at
Luke. A slow dawning of recognition began to creep
across his face. "Wait a minute," he said slowly. "Luke
Chisholm? Aren't you . . . didn't you play defensive back
for the 49ers a few years ago?"

Luke nodded casually.

"Oh, hey. Hey Jean, look at him!" He pointed toward
the couch. "It's Luke Chisholm." Suddenly he seemed
even younger and full of awed pleasure. He sat down
eagerly on the edge of the couch, his gaze full of Luke as
though he'd found his hero. "I saw you in the play-offs
that last year. That was a great stop you made on Balan-
koff."

Luke smiled. "Too bad I didn't do it often enough to
keep them from winning the game."

"Yeah, but the 49ers would've won if you hadn't been
injured in the third quarter."

Luke's smile was modest. "We'll never know. That
was the last shot my knee took and it just about finished
me in football."

Jean stood at the side of the room, watching them.
They'd forgotten all about her, she realized suddenly.
Just a moment before she'd been the center of a tug-of-
war between two males, a position she'd never been in
before, and though it had been a little scary, she had to
admit it had been sort of exciting, too. And now that
they'd found football in common, she'd been tossed
aside.

Her first twinge of resentment gave way to amusement as she noted the hero worship in Jeffrey's eyes.

She'd never known he was such a sports fan. She frowned. Maybe there was a lot she didn't know about Jeffrey. How could she have gone so long with a man she really knew nothing about? Could it be because she just hadn't cared enough to find out?

Her glance shifted to Luke and suddenly she knew she cared very much about him, about what he liked and didn't like, about where he'd come from and where he was going, about why he'd hurt his knee, about whether or not he had a girlfriend. She felt heat rising in her cheeks. *Oh, Jean,* she told herself pleadingly, *don't do this to yourself.*

3

"Put on something glamorous, Jean." Luke's husky drawl jolted her back to the scene at hand. "Jeffrey's agreed to go with us after all."

She bit her lip as she retreated into her bedroom. She'd noticed how he'd turned the evening into something between him and her, with Jeffrey the tagalong instead of the other way around. But she didn't care. She was going to see him for a few hours longer and that was enough at this point.

Put on something glamorous, he'd said. She pulled open the double doors to her closet, knowing that she would find mostly pullover shirts and sweaters, with a few nicely pressed slacks in coordinated colors and little else. What on earth could she wear that was the least bit glamorous?

She slid the wire hangers across the metal pole, growing more and more anxious as she eliminated one thing after another. She didn't have one decent dress in her whole wardrobe.

Then her gaze fell on something squashed against the very back of her closet. The colors were peach and pink, in swirls on a slinky material, and at first she didn't recognize what it was. Reaching in, she pulled the garment out and laid it across her bed.

She remembered the dress now. She'd bought it almost two years ago in a sudden burst of exuberance over a win at an international meet. When she'd tried it on in the hotel boutique, the saleswoman had told her that the style did wonderful things for her.

"It makes you look like a woman," she'd said, nodding knowingly. "It gives you curves, honey, and God knows you could use some."

Jean hadn't been offended. She was used to such comments. She'd bought the dress on a cloud of hope, but when she'd tried it on at home the hope had faded.

What had seemed fun and slightly daring in the shop, looked silly and out-of-place in the long mirror in her bedroom. The reflection that had stared out at her wore a woebegone look, like a little girl dressed up in her mother's clothes. The dress had been all wrong. She'd never worn it.

But right now there wasn't much choice; there simply wasn't anything else. Gritting her teeth, she slipped out of her jump suit and pulled the filmy dress over her head.

The material rustled crisply as she pulled it into place. It seemed snugger than it had when she'd bought it. Perhaps she'd gained a little weight.

Swinging around, she looked into her mirror. Eyes wide, she gazed at what she saw there, wondering if this could possibly be the same dress she'd shunted away into the dark recesses of her closet.

The bodice of the light dress was gathered and it hugged tightly, pushing up her small breasts so that the soft curve of them showed attractively above the neckline. The sleeves were full and bloused about the wrists. Her tan skin was a creamy mocha against the pastel colors of the fabric, and her legs looked strong and muscular under the clinging folds of the knee-length skirt.

Gazing into the mirror, she could hardly believe this was Jean Archer she saw before her. Taking up her silver-backed brush, she ran it through her hair until it shone, noticing for the first time the sun-kissed glint of gold in her tawny tresses.

She slipped her feet into white sandals and walked slowly back out into the living room, not sure what to expect.

"Wow!" Jeffrey's reaction was gratifying. "Jean, is that really you?" His smile was pleased, as though he'd had something to do with her perceived transformation. "Doesn't she look great?" he asked Luke.

Jean turned to look at Luke, hoping for a similar response, but what she found was like a dash of cold water. Luke's eyes were as cold as blue ice. His thick russet eyebrows were pulled together as though something about her didn't please him at all. "Yes, she looks great," he answered, but Jean could tell his heart wasn't in it.

Her first wave of hurt disappointment was followed by a splash of anger, mostly at herself for caring so much. She grumbled internally as she gathered together her purse and prepared to leave with the two men. She'd always stood on her own before. She'd never needed a man's approval. If she let herself fall prey to that sort of thing now, there'd be nothing but heartbreak ahead.

They drove to the Strip in Jeffrey's Cutlass, all sitting in the front seat with Jean in the middle. The spring evening was still glowing with the stark desert light and the crowds were out on the sidewalks, walking from one casino to another, deciding which restaurant to eat at.

"You're staying at the Camelot?" Jean asked as they swung into the parking lot. "I guess making footballs pays a pretty good salary." She wondered vaguely what part he hoped to have her play in the game.

He didn't answer, instead directing Jeffrey to pull up before the lavish front of the hotel rather than going on to a parking space. The warmth between the two of them had fled ever since she'd walked out in her pretty dress, and she couldn't imagine what had caused the frost. She only knew she didn't like it.

"Mr. Chisholm," the valet said, almost saluting like a buck private to a four-star general. "Would you like me to take care of this car for your friend?"

"Thanks, Bobby." Luke's smile returned as he faced the young man. "I'd appreciate it."

Jeffrey looked after his precious Cutlass as though he wasn't sure where the valet might take it. "Is that guy bonded?" he muttered warily, turning to follow Luke with reluctance.

"Don't worry, Jeff," Jean reassured him, casting a sidelong look at their host. "I'm sure Luke will buy you a new car if that one gets dented." She was hoping to get a rise out of Luke, still uncertain why his mood had shifted as it had.

His blue eyes flashed her way knowingly. "Sure," he answered smoothly. "I'll buy him two, one for each foot."

She sighed with exaggerated happiness. "Rich people are so much fun. Don't you think so, Jeffrey?"

"I don't know," he replied, bobbing his head at the doorman who held the massive glass door for them to enter the opulent lobby. "I've never known any before. I think I'll reserve judgment." He looked at her questioningly. "Besides, how do we know this guy is rich?" He grinned at Luke.

"Only rich people stay at the Camelot," she answered, as though Luke wasn't walking alongside them. "I'm willing to bet he's loaded." She looked up at Luke through her lashes. "Are you loaded, Luke?"

His smile was wide now, though he wouldn't look her in the eye. "I'm beginning to feel like I've saddled myself with the Katzenjammer kids here," he muttered, putting a hand behind Jean's back to steer her into the huge casino area. "Do you two go on like this all the time?"

"Constantly," Jean replied, and suddenly she realized it was true. She and Jeffrey had always been more like a couple of mischievous kids when they got together than like a pair of sweethearts. There'd never been any real spark of passion between them, just warm friendship. She'd never felt the lack until today.

The royal purple carpeting was lush beneath their feet, and though the floor of the casino was lined with silver slot machines and felt-covered gaming tables, just as it was in any other casino, the walls were hung with tapestries, and huge crystal chandeliers were lowered from the high ceiling, giving the place an aspect that was half medieval castle, half opera house. Statues of King Arthur and all the Knights of the Round Table were placed at intervals along the walls. As each statue was at least twenty feet high, the characters seemed to brood over the scene. Jean had wondered, each of the few times she'd been here, if they really approved of what went on below them.

"Are you taking us to the Avalon Room?" Jean guessed, knowing that was the nicest dining room in the hotel.

Luke looked down at her, his faint smile mysterious. "No," was his only reply.

He strode along with quick grace and she noticed his leg seemed not to bother him at all. *A remarkably good recovery*, she thought to herself. She might even be suspicious of it if she hadn't seen the scars he carried with him.

They climbed the wide stairway to the rotunda where a huge marble statue of the Lady Guinevere stood, her head lowered in melancholy regret.

"Either she lost the rent money at the tables," Jeffrey

quipped with an elbow into Jean's ribs, "or she's just eaten the food. Let's hope it's the first one."

Jean moved away from him, finally a bit uncomfortable with his silly humor. Luke was right, they did sound like cartoon characters. She didn't want him to think of her that way.

As they walked quickly past the fashionable shops she began to wonder if Luke could possibly be taking them to his room. She was about to ask him when they came to a stop before a man in a tuxedo who stood guarding an unmarked door.

"I'd like to take two guests in," Luke told the man calmly. "I realize I'm not dressed properly, but perhaps you can make an exception tonight."

The man's smile was genuine. "Of course, Mr. Chisholm. Come right this way."

The door opened and they were swallowed up by a velvet blackness, eased only by an occasional candle that flickered over a linen tablecloth like a diamond set against the night. Eerie faces floated above the candlelight as the patrons ate their dinner, adding to the mysterious atmosphere.

"Wow," Jeffrey breathed into her ear. "Get a load of this. There's even a dungeon in Camelot."

The three of them moved cautiously until their eyes grew more accustomed to the dark. The man in the tuxedo pulled out a chair for Jean, lit a candle, and suddenly they had their own table with its small circle of light to hold them in its spell.

"What is this place?" Jean asked Luke as he sat beside her. "I feel as though I've descended into an ancient cave dwelling."

"A place for little beasties," Jeffrey chimed in. "Dwarfs and leprechauns. I wouldn't be surprised to see the shoemaker and his elves march through, tapping our knees with their little hammers as they go."

Jean turned toward her friend, half exasperated, half intrigued. "Why on earth would they want to tap our knees with their little hammers?" she asked curiously.

"I don't know." Jeffrey shrugged, face utterly blank. "You'll have to ask them."

Jean turned away with a moan, but Luke laughed. She looked quickly into his face, finding the warmth she'd hoped for. "This is called Pendragon's Tomb," he told them. "It's a private club."

"For high rollers?" Jean guessed, wondering if that was what Luke Chisholm was all about.

"Not exclusively."

A waiter appeared beside the table as though by magic and offered Luke a wine list. He was dressed in black tails and a white shirt so crisp it seemed to have a life of its own.

"It's nice to see this place is an equal opportunity employer," Jeffrey said with a remarkably straight face. "I hate a place that discriminates against penguins."

Luke ignored him, glancing around the table questioningly. "Do either of you have a preference? If not, I'd like to suggest the house Chardonnay."

Jeffrey shrugged. "I suppose they're out of Thundernectar, so why not?"

Jean glared at him, then glanced at Luke. "That will be fine," she said softly.

The waiter returned quickly, presented the bottle to Luke to examine, then pulled the cork with a flourish. He poured a bit in Luke's glass and waited for him to take a sip and approve or disapprove.

Instead of doing it himself, Luke handed the glass to Jean. "It's up to you," he told her smoothly. "Is it wine or is it vinegar?"

She started to refuse the honor, since she knew absolutely nothing about judging and presumed that Luke knew a lot. But she caught the sparkle in his eyes and knew he wasn't going to allow her to back out. So she put the crystal glass to her lips and let the golden liquid flow onto her tongue.

She rolled it around in her mouth, pretending to consider thoughtfully, trying frantically to remember the words people used to describe wines.

It was hard to swallow with everyone staring at her. "A delightful wine," she said approvingly, though to her ears her voice came out a stiff croak. "Dry enough to whet the appetite, full-bodied enough to satisfy." She looked around anxiously, hoping she hadn't made a complete fool of herself.

Luke's smile was reassurance enough. "Fine," he said, turning back to the waiter. "You may pour the wine."

Jean glowed with pleasure, then began to hope she'd been right. If Luke took one sip and choked, she'd know she was in trouble. The waiter completed the pouring and left the bottle in ice beside the table. She watched Luke anxiously. When was he going to taste the wine?

Meanwhile Jeffrey was growing weary of being ignored. "I've heard about this place," he said slowly, peering around in the gloom. "A lot of people who'd rather not be seen in public eat here."

Luke's grin included them both. "In that case, it might be better if you stopped trying to see them," he advised.

"Oh." Jeffrey grimaced, pulling in his head like a turtle. "I guess you're right."

Luke raised his glass and the other two did likewise. "To Las Vegas, with all its contradictions," he toasted.

"And just what is that supposed to mean?" Jean asked, still holding her glass aloft, trying to put off the moment when Luke would taste the wine.

His smile was endearingly crooked and this time it

was just for her. "That means that I never expected to find a gem like you among all the rhinestones that coat this place."

"Oh." She didn't know whether to be pleased for herself or offended for her city. He made her uncomfortable in a deliciously exotic way and she hadn't decided yet if she liked it or not.

She watched as he drank from his glass, trying to read the reaction in his eyes. "Delicious," he told her softly, and she let out a relieved sigh, then turned away, embarrassed that he'd realized how anxious she was.

Still, she felt wonderful sitting beside him. She felt a very different person from the woman who'd first met him in the late afternoon. Maybe it was the dress, making her feel as though she was almost pretty and certainly feminine. Or maybe it was this handsome man sitting beside her, casting glances her way that seemed to touch her with an almost tactile force.

He liked what he saw when he looked at her. She could tell by the gleam in his gaze, the way the laugh lines around his eyes deepened, the way his mouth turned up at the corners. If she wasn't careful she might almost begin to feel beautiful.

As it was she felt light as a feather, sailing on the current of his interest. She looked at Jeffrey and was surprised to see that he looked much the same. Suddenly she felt a sliver of dread. Was this all an act? Was this just Luke's natural charm at work, making everyone within earshot fall all over him?

Slightly wary, she raised her glass again. "Do we get menus?" she asked as she sipped her wine.

"No," Luke answered. "They serve one menu every night, take it or leave it."

The meal began with asparagus soup lightly laced with tarragon. It picked up speed through the shrimp in dill and on into the main course, which consisted of sliced duck served with papaya wedges in a tart lemon sauce.

Jean loved the patina of mellow light that tinged the scene as the candle flickered in the gloom. She enjoyed the beautiful food and the classic service, but she had trouble eating anything. There seemed to be a barrier in her throat that wouldn't let food down.

Luke and Jeffrey ate with relish and spent most of the time between bites talking about football.

"What a life that must've been," Jeffrey said enviously, drinking wine with a flourish. "On television every Sunday, playing the most macho game around and doing it well, girls hanging around the locker-room door, movie stars waiting in your hotel room—"

"And then there's Monday morning," Luke broke in sardonically, "when your body won't work and the pain makes you want to stay in bed for the week, and the coach is on the phone yelling about the mistakes you made, and the girl who seemed so loving and beautiful the night before looks like a headhunter with another scalp on her belt, anxious to leave and tell all her friends about her conquest." He shook his head. "It's not all roses, my friend."

Jeffrey was unconvinced. "Yeah, but you loved it, right?"

Jean watched as Luke let his conflicting emotions show on his face. "I loved the game," he said slowly. "I didn't love everything that came with it."

"You didn't let it become your whole life then," Jeffrey said wisely. "Not like Jean does her diving."

Jean froze, staring at Jeffrey. There'd been a twinge of bitterness in his tone that was unmistakable. She'd never realized he'd cared that much. He'd known from the beginning how much diving meant to her. She'd never lied about it.

He didn't meet her eyes. Instead he speared another piece of golden papaya on the tines of his fork and popped it into his mouth. Whatever he might have felt about her single-mindedness at one time, it seemed he no longer resented it enough to try and change her.

She looked at Luke and found him studying her.

"Don't you like it?" he asked, gesturing toward her uneaten meal. "I'll have the waiter bring you something else."

"No," she answered hurriedly. "Oh, no. It . . . it's just so pretty I hate to spoil the display." She dutifully took a bit of duck into her mouth and chewed energetically.

Jeffrey spoke again, turning Luke's mind back to football, and Jean watched the two of them while she tried to swallow her food.

Suddenly memories of fifteen years earlier flooded her. She'd been in a restaurant very similar to this, except it was in a hotel downtown, the Golden Palace. Her Uncle Max had taken her there for her thirteenth birthday, and he'd plied her with steak and lobster before setting a three-tiered sundae in front of her.

"It's your special day, babe," he'd told her. "You can have anything you want."

She smiled as she thought of Uncle Max. He was her mother's brother and her father had never approved of him very much.

"We're decent hardworking folks, Jean," he would tell her when another visit from Max was imminent. "We don't need fancy frills like that uncle of yours."

Max had money and the Archers never had more than enough to scrape by. Jean's father had owned a furniture store. He was decent, as he said, honest and hardworking. But he never could get ahead.

Max, on the other hand, seemed to float through life on an ocean of fun. He was a professional poker player who traveled the gambler's circuit, playing in tournaments all over the world. Whenever he stopped in Las Vegas, he had chocolates for her mother and silver coins for Jean. He could make a dime disappear in his hand and come out in his ear. Jean would ask to see that trick again and again, but she never could catch him making the switch. Deep down inside, she really believed it was magic that did it.

Uncle Max *was* magic. He carried an aura of excitement that was missing from her ordinary life. He was the one who paid for the summer camp for Jean when she was fourteen, the camp where she first tried diving, first felt what it was to be a bird soaring through the air.

"That's better."

She looked up, surprised to find Luke smiling at her approvingly.

"You're eating," he explained, and she looked down, amazed to see that she'd almost cleaned her plate. "Are you going to have room for dessert?" He reached out to smooth back a strand of her hair that was flying out from the rest and she felt the tingle his touch created run across her skin. "Or shall we save desert for later?" he asked huskily, and she read the meaning in his eyes.

She flushed, suddenly feeling very awkward, glancing at Jeffrey to see if he'd heard. But her friend was engrossed in emptying the condiment tray of olives and pickled onions. "Tell me about the Super Bowl game," he said, oblivious to the current flowing between the other two. "Was it really as exciting as it looked on TV?"

Luke turned away from her with seeming reluctance and answered Jeffrey, but she didn't pay attention to what he was saying. She retreated into the past again, remembering how it had been at the camp where she'd learned the basics of diving.

She'd been terrified when the counselor had forced

her to go up on the board for the first time. She'd never considered herself much of an athlete and she'd tried to get out of it.

"Come on, Jean," the young counselor had coaxed. "You've got to try everything once. How will you know whether you like it or not if you've never tried it?"

The others were watching, snickering. She hadn't made many friends and she was an outsider to them. They'd never forget it if she chickened out. She knew she had to do it.

Gathering all her courage, she'd stepped up onto the board and walked shakily out to the end. The cloth felt slippery beneath her feet and the water looked so very far away. She'd stared down at the sparkling depths, her breath coming faster. Her muscles were frozen with fear. She couldn't do it.

"What's the matter, Jean? The board too high? The water too cold?" The laughter was getting louder.

"Don't listen to them, Jean" The counselor's voice had cut through the giggling. "Just listen to yourself. You can do it. The power is in you."

Jean had closed her eyes, blocking out everything but the sound of her own breathing. Using every bit of will-power she possessed, she had put her arms over her head and pushed off with her toes.

The feeling had been incredible. It was as though she'd launched herself into another world. For just a few seconds, she had been flying. The air was around her like a comforting caress. Her body was long and stretched as she never dared stretch it on land. Then she broke the surface and plunged down into the cool velvet water. She'd found a home at last, somewhere she felt she belonged. She would never forget that first feeling of overwhelming joy.

When she had climbed back out of the pool, no one

had to encourage her to try it again. She ran around to the line at the back of the board. Again and again she had dove, hardly noticing as the murmuring around her began to include words like "natural ability" and "swan-like grace." She wasn't diving for them. She was doing it for herself.

Jeffrey was right when he said that diving was her whole life. It had been right from that day. What might have happened to her if Eleanor hadn't insisted she try it?

It was Eleanor, her coach, who'd been that camp counselor on that fateful day. She sometimes wondered if Eleanor had instinctively known there was a diver hiding inside her shy awkward body. Eleanor herself had been working at the camp to make enough money to compete at the Olympic diving trials the following year. Little did they both know that a lifetime of partnership lay ahead of them.

"More wine?" Luke was looking at her again. In this candlelight he almost reminded her of Uncle Max.

"No, thanks. I'm in training."

Luke put down the bottle and tilted his head back, looking across the table. "Jeffrey," he said softly, "I'm going to ask you an impertinent question, but I seriously need an answer."

"Fire away," Jeffrey replied carelessly, gulping down more wine. "Impertinence is my specialty."

Luke leaned forward on his elbows. "Just what are your intentions as far as Jean is concerned?" he asked quietly, as though it was a perfectly normal question.

Jean gasped. For some reason she began to tremble as though this moment was crucial.

Jeffrey looked thunderstruck. Then he seemed to come to the conclusion that Luke was joking. "My intentions?" he repeated, wide-eyed. "Do you mean that in the old-fashioned sense?"

Luke's mouth twisted in a half smile. "Exactly," he replied.

"Honorable, of course." He struck himself stoutly across the chest. "There's not a more honorable man in all of England."

This time Luke didn't smile. "That's not enough," he said. "You see, I intend to make Jean a proposition she won't be able to refuse, and I want to make sure she'll be free to accept it."

The business proposition. She'd forgotten it again. What on earth did he have in mind that could be so serious? "Just what is it you want me to do?" she asked with quick curiosity.

He didn't look at her. He was still watching Jeffrey, gauging his reaction. "Later," he told her softly. "I want to see where Jeffrey stands right now."

Jeffrey was leaning forward, placing his wineglass on the table so carefully Jean knew he'd had a little too much of the contents.

"You know, Luke," he said seriously, "I'm going to be straight with you. I'm going to tell you the truth."

"Is that right?" Jean asked, slightly miffed at the way the two of them were discussing her. "Will it be the same truth you've always told me?"

He narrowed his eyes and waved a finger at her. "You know as well as I do where we stand. I'm married to my career. What I need is a wife who'll marry it, too. I hoped for a while, with your physical therapy training...." His voice trailed off as he shook his head. "But we both know that won't work. Not while you're involved in diving."

He chuckled and reached for the wineglass again. "Diving always came first, physical therapy was second, and once in a while I felt like I rated a distant third. But not often."

Jean hugged her arms in tight, feeling cold. She knew there was a lot of truth in what Jeffrey was saying, even if her first impulse was to deny it. Diving was the most important thing in her life. It had been ever since she found it was the one place where she could be beautiful, where she could shine. She had no other place for that. She couldn't give it up, not for Jeffrey.

"Thank you, Jeffrey," Luke said in a low rumbling tone. "I appreciate your candor." He looked at Jean. "So you won't mind if I do what I can to win her for myself."

Jean frowned, her eyes searching his. The way he put it, she might almost think he was planning a campaign of seduction. But she knew better, or at least she thought she did. He wanted her for some sort of business deal, probably an advertising contract. This was only a very grandstanding sort of play to capture her imagination.

She had to admit he'd done rather a good job of that. As she sat beside him, she was very much aware of him as a man in a way she never was with any other man she knew. Every time he moved, she seemed to sense it with more than just sight. She felt it, tasted it, heard it. She could close her eyes and still know what he was doing at any given moment. And right now she could feel a tension in him that went beyond simple business maneuvering. The sense of it set off an excitement in her that was as thrilling as a glass of bubbly champagne.

"Carry on, Luke, my friend," Jeffrey was saying, waving his wineglass grandly in the air. "You're a better man than I am if you can woo her from the three-meter board. Good luck to you."

Jean felt a rush of uneasy emotion. They were bargaining for her as though she were a bag of potatoes! Holding back the sharp words that rose in her throat, she carefully laid down her fork and wiped her mouth with her napkin, preparing to tell them exactly what she thought of them both, in as ladylike a fashion as she could manage under the circumstances.

But before she had a chance to do just that, a strange electronic noise stopped them all.

"My beeper," Jeffrey explained apologetically, fumbling in his pocket to turn the device off. "Rats. I was afraid of this."

He looked around a bit helplessly and Luke interceded, gesturing for the waiter. "May we please have a telephone?" he asked quietly.

"Right here at the table?" Jeffrey asked. "Wow, this is a classy place."

The telephone arrived and was placed discreetly at his elbow. Jeffrey picked up the receiver and dialed an outside line, then contacted his service.

While he talked, Jean leaned closer to Luke. "If he has to go to the hospital, I'll have to take him," she said softly. "He's in no condition to take himself."

Luke raised one eyebrow. "Are you looking for an excuse to escape?" he asked.

She flushed. "Of course not." Not at all. In fact, she could think of few things she would like better than to spend more time with him. "But Jeffrey's had a bit too much wine. Can't you see that? And he shouldn't be behind the wheel of a car."

Luke searched her eyes. His own reflected the flicker of the candlelight. "Don't worry about it," he told her. "I'll take care of him."

Before Jean could ask just how he planned to do that, Jeffrey was off the phone. "Emergency," he said glibly. "Got a lady expecting twins on her way in from north of Lake Mead. Gotta go."

He stood, weaving a bit. "Goodbye you two. Have a nice evening."

Luke rose with him. "Wait here," he told Jean with a wink. "I'll be right back."

She sighed as she watched the two of them walk off, watched the darkness envelope them. She didn't know exactly why, but she just naturally wanted to do what Luke Chisholm told her to do. She would have to fight that impulse.

She thought over what Jeffrey had said and knew he'd told the truth. The only thing that surprised her was that he hadn't been happy with their relationship. She had. It had suited her ideally—just enough closeness to keep loneliness at bay, but enough distance and independence to leave her time to concentrate on her real love—diving.

That sort of space was essential for a champion. Without it, concentration was diffused and the championship drifted further and further beyond reach. She'd had Jeffrey and her freedom as well. She hadn't realized he'd wanted something more.

But Luke...she knew instinctively that he would never settle for a relationship such as the one she'd had with Jeffrey. He'd demand center stage, no matter what. No one could love a man like Luke and still be a champion. No one.

He was back very quickly, sinking into the chair beside her with a brief smile in her direction. "Don't worry about Jeffrey," he reassured her. "I'm having someone drive him over to the hospital, plying him with coffee all the way. He'll stay with him until he's sure the effects of the wine have worn off completely. He'll probably have quite a wait for that patient."

She stared at him, willing herself to see him clearly with no emotions clouding the picture. "You take care of everything. don't you?" she said, her voice almost accusing. "You just snap your fingers and the world jumps into order for you."

His grin was endearingly lopsided, but she steeled herself against its charm. "Hardly," he said. "Sometimes it takes a stiff kick to get everyone in line."

She raised her chin challengingly. "You'd better not kick me, Luke Chisholm," she warned. "I just might have a nasty countermove."

Leaning back in his chair, he chuckled as though she'd said something very amusing. "I'll bet you do, Jean," he agreed. "I'll just bet you do."

Nervously, she avoided his eyes, playing with her silverware instead of looking at him. She hardly noticed the waiter who silently removed their dishes, then returned with coffee and a tray of flavorings to go with it.

"What do you prefer?" Luke asked casually. "We have cinnamon." He lifted the tiny silver spoon to let the brown spice sift back down into the porcelain bowl it came in. "Or we have chocolate." He held up a little stick of dark chocolate. "There's whipped cream and brandy. What should I add to your cup?"

She knew she wouldn't be able to drink a thing. The barrier was back in her throat. She wanted to escape from this man and all the terrifying emotions he set loose in her.

"I like it black," she told him shortly. "You said you wanted to talk business. Why don't we get down to it?"

He frowned as though affronted. "Not yet, Jean," he said, his voice as smooth as the brandy he was adding to her cup. "We need to relax. I'm going to fix up your coffee the way I like mine. If you don't care for it, I'll order you another cup and leave it black."

He put a thin stick of chocolate into her drink and the two of them watched it slowly dissolve.

Jean decided to let his high-handed manner pass. After all, she wasn't going to drink the liquid no matter what he put in it. She only wanted the time to pass quickly so she could get out of here and back to her own home, away from the pitfalls she felt all around her when she was with Luke.

"I should be getting home," she began. "I've got to be at practice early in the morning."

"No." She looked up in surprise to find him shaking his head, laughing down at her. "No, you're not going to get away from me so easily, Jean."

She could have sworn he was closer than before, even if she hadn't seen him move his chair. Suddenly his hand was at the nape of her neck, holding her in a gentle grip, but turning her resolutely toward him.

"What are you afraid of, Jean?" he asked, his gaze moving across her face, searching out every shadow in the golden light. "When I met you this afternoon, you were a sassy wisecracker. You took me home and stripped the pants right off me."

"I did not!" But she knew he was only trying to get a rise out of her.

She risked a quick look into his eyes. His grin was wide and teasing.

"Then you put on this dress and turn into a vision that takes my breath away and makes me think about scary things."

She gazed at him wide-eyed. So that was why he'd gone cold when she had walked into the room all dressed up. But that was ridiculous. He was implying that the feelings she'd evoked had scared him. Surely he was joking.

"Now you've gone back into your trembling virgin act," he continued, shaking his head. "I like the other Jean Archer much better."

He was right. She was acting like a ninny. She could stand up to anything he could do to her. She knew what her goals were.

"I'm not afraid of you," she said stoutly, looking him in the eye. "I'm not afraid of anyone."

"Good." He gestured toward the waiter, who arrived with a chit for him to sign. Dispensing with that, Luke rose, forcing her up with him. "Then let's get out of here, shall we?"

His hand slipped to the small of her back as they left the room and went out into the brightly lit corridor. The fingers pressed slightly into her flesh and she had to fight back the urge to arch into his touch.

"Where are we going?" she asked sharply, ready to fend off an attempt to take her up to his room.

"Dancing," he said, steering her along briskly. "I want to hold you in my arms and something tells me I'm going to have to have a good excuse for that tonight. So we're going dancing."

"DANCING?" Jean tried to pull away from his hand but his arm slid around her waist, holding her close as they walked. She felt the warmth of him through the thin cloth of her dress. She couldn't dance with him. She knew instinctively that moving against his body to a slow and sultry melody would be little short of blatant lovemaking. The thought of it filled her with dread.

"You can't go dancing with that knee," she told him as sternly as she could manage. "You'll destroy it."

"Then you'll have to fix me up again." He guided her down a darkened hallway and into a room from which music was drifting. Inside, the lights were low, except for the sparkling color of disco bulbs that blinked at intervals from the ceiling. The music had a strong beat, but it was more tuneful than noisy. Luke led her out onto the dance floor.

"I...I don't really know much about dancing," she said, making a last-ditch effort at avoiding what she knew was to come.

"Don't be ridiculous," he said, accepting no excuses. "Every dive is ballet in the air. You have perfect timing. You can dance."

As it turned out, it didn't matter much whether she knew how to dance or not. With Luke to lead the way, all she had to do was follow, born along in his strong embrace. She might have closed her eyes and abandoned herself to him and still found herself moving to the rhythm.

Her heart was beating so loudly she could hardly tell it from the downbeat in the music. Her head felt light, and as Luke turned to face her, his arms sliding around her as though to pick her up and carry her away, she felt herself surrender.

His potent energy wrapped around her like a desert wind, bearing her up in its power. The lights began to blur as he spun her, the music faded into a sound from far away, an echo of another time, another place.

She never noticed if there were others on the floor, even if there were others in the room. As they swayed and turned, she was aware only of his presence and that was all she cared about.

The length of his leg as it strained against her thigh, the hint of his warm dark scent as it came to her from inside his open shirt, the tingle of his breath against her skin, and when he leaned down to whisper in her ear, the roughness of his evening beard against her cheek—everything about him sent the blood rushing through her, leaving her as light-headed as if she'd drunk all the wine herself.

"You see," he told her softly, pulling her closer against him, "your dancing is terrific."

"Your dancing is what's terrific," she answered almost groggily. "Mine is just superfluous in its wake."

"Why do you do that all the time?" He stopped dead, turning her face up to meet his gaze with a finger under her chin. "Why do you put yourself down?"

She tried to avoid his eyes, embarrassed. She knew exactly why, but she wasn't about to tell him. She did it to beat others to the punch. If you got your own self-deprecatory remarks in quickly, others might not bother to make any.

"I don't want to hear you do it again," he told her, his voice hard with calm authority. "If you do it too much you'll start to believe it yourself."

First he tried to tell her she was beautiful, now he wanted her to believe she was a marvelous dancer. Jean began to wonder if the man enjoyed living in a dream-world, or if reality was just too much of a downer for him to take without sugar coating.

She liked to consider herself a realist. She knew the score and was ready to face the consequences. Even so, she let him pull her back against his chest, and this time she let her head press in where his shirt opened, first to hide the color in her cheeks, and then to savor the warmth of him.

The room receded again and she tried to maintain her equilibrium, straining to keep from falling under the spell. It was no use, and soon she gave up the attempt. She was floating above the floor and all she had to hold onto was the man in her arms.

His hands seemed to burn through the thin material covering her back. She could sense the warmth of his breath in her hair, and then he bent down to press his lips to the slope of her neck and she closed her eyes, letting the tingle grow.

"You smell like a sunny morning," he whispered into the hollow behind her ear.

Despite her delicious languour, she began to chuckle. "I smell like a swimming pool and you know it," she retorted, nestling against him as though it was her natural place. "I've been wearing Eau de Chlorine most of my life."

His arms tightened around her and he nibbled warningly on the tender tip of her earlobe. "You're doing it again," he accused. "Let a compliment stand on its own without any qualifying comments."

She sighed. "I'll be glad to, as long as the compliment tells the truth."

"Truth," he growled, leading her slowly toward the side of the room. "Since when are you so interested in truth?"

She let him guide her where he wanted to go, without looking or commenting. She could hear the music growing fainter, but she didn't bother to open her eyes to see where they were headed.

"I've always been interested in truth," she murmured. "I hate lies."

The air hitting her skin was cool now and she knew they were outside, but still she hid her face against his chest, letting him take command, swaying with him to the faraway beat of the music.

"What do you call the ruse you used to keep me from talking to you this afternoon in the information office?" he asked teasingly. "Was that 'truth'?"

Finally she drew back, looking up at him. "You did know! Bette thought you did." She grinned. "I told her you were guessing."

"I knew." They'd stopped moving but he held her as though they were still dancing. He was looking down at her with a light in his eyes that sent a shiver down the length of her back to her tailbone. Suddenly she was apprehensive. It wasn't that she thought he might do anything to harm her; she knew he had no such intention. But she detected something in the depths of his eyes that went beyond simple attraction, and she wished she hadn't seen it at all.

"Jean...." he began, cupping her cheek with one hand, and she jerked away, pulling herself out of his embrace and turning nervously to look at their setting.

"What is this, a terrace?" she asked quickly, taking a

few steps across the flagstones as though to explore it. "We're certainly all alone out here."

Tables and chairs were pushed to the side, as though this area was in use during the warm afternoons, but the early spring nights were still too cool for most people. She could hear the music from inside, drifting out the French doors they must have come through, but no one else had been intrepid enough to follow them.

"Jean." He erased the distance between them with two giant strides and she shrank back against the cold stone of the building.

He wouldn't let her escape. Putting one arm on either side of her head, he leaned against the wall himself, holding her prisoner. "We were talking about truth."

"Truth?" she echoed stupidly. "Were we?"

"We were." He put one hand under her chin, forcing her to meet his dark gaze. "And you were about to tell me some."

Her throat felt dry and raspy. He looked so incredibly handsome with the moonlight making dark shadows across his face. "What, exactly, do you want to know?"

His fingers traveled down to her neck, sliding softly up and down the silky column. "You heard the question I asked Jeffrey. You heard me tell him I intended to take over your life."

She nodded, wide-eyed. "You were joking, weren't you?"

He leaned down closer so that his breath tickled her nose, while he studied every line and curve of her face as though it were an art object he was thinking of collecting. "No, Jean," he said simply. "You and Jeffrey may make life into a running gag, but I don't. I meant exactly what I said."

She ran her tongue across her dry lips. "I think Jeffrey took it as a joke," she told him weakly.

He shrugged negligently. "That's his problem. I told him my intentions. My conscience is clear." His fingers dug in slightly as he held her head still while he dropped a slow kiss on her mouth.

"The only thing I need to know now," he whispered huskily between more kisses, "is what you think about it." His tongue traced a line of hot sensation across the trembling line between her lips, urging it to open to his penetration.

"Tell me, Jean," he coaxed. "Or better yet, show me."

His mouth on hers was fierce persuasion, forcing apart her lips and entering to test the response inside. Jean felt as though she had no will of her own any longer, as though she was made for nothing but this, to fit against this man, to love and be loved.

His body pressed into hers, forcing her back against the wall, touching every part of her, introducing her to a wealth of feeling that took her breath away.

She found her arms curling up around his neck, hands reaching for his well-muscled back. Frustrated by the thickness of cloth that kept the warmth of his body from her, she drew her hands back down and reached in under the suit coat, sliding her fingers along the ridges of his hard stomach.

Suddenly his hand was covering hers, guiding her even further, showing her how to slip under the shirt to find the real source of his heat. She gasped as she felt him shudder beneath her touch. It gave her an odd feeling of power, mixed liberally with wonder, that she could make him react with such intensity.

"That's it, Jean," he told her, his voice thick with an emotion that made her pulse race. "That's what I want to know."

What was she telling him, she wondered hazily, not

about to stop, whatever it was. What was he reading from her actions?

She knew she ought to pause and assess what was happening here, but she couldn't. She'd never felt such excitement, such pure golden joy as she felt with Luke's hands on her body, his mouth making a trail of shimmering kisses down across the nape of her neck. No other man had ever awakened her this way. She had a sudden intuition that no other man ever would.

She'd known Luke for only a few hours, and yet she was sure he'd changed her life. He said he didn't joke, that when he said he was taking over, he meant it. The thought thrilled her now. It didn't scare her as it had at first.

She'd been infatuated before. She'd even thought she might be in love. But this was something more than she'd ever known. How could one man make such a difference so quickly? Was this love? Could she have fallen in love so quickly? This time was it the real thing?

No. It was impossible. And yet she was attracted to him as she'd never been attracted to a man before.

"You don't love Jeffrey, do you?" he demanded with a rough insistence. "Tell me that you don't."

Showing him obviously wasn't enough after all. She pulled open two buttons on his shirt before answering his request. "I don't love Jeffrey," she agreed softly. "We've never been much more than good friends."

He frowned as though he hardly knew whether to believe her. "I feel like a hypocrite," he muttered, more to himself than to her, "but suddenly that's very important to me."

She pressed back the sides of his shirt, then touched the wiry dark hair that curled on his strong chest. She'd never considered herself a particularly passionate woman. She'd never taken the initiative, never even wanted to. Instinctively, she knew she wanted to now. It felt so right, and she was so very brave tonight, as though a special courage flowed through her, a courage ignited by the fire in his eyes.

"Jeffrey and I have passed the time when we might have made more out of our relationship," she told him, realizing as she said it just how true it was. "He wasn't joking when he said he was married to his career and I was immersed in mine. Diving has always come first with me."

Her fingertips dipped beneath the carpet of fur and felt for the jolting beat of his heart. It thumped beneath her hand like a thing with a life of its own and she pressed closer to it, wanting to merge her pulse with his. He threw back his head and narrowed his eyes as she caressed him, watching her with a look that held a certain fierceness.

"Diving isn't going to come first anymore," he told her firmly. "I'm afraid you're about to make a big change in your life."

His words sent a stabbing shock through her, but she stifled it immediately. He didn't know what he was talking about. Diving would always come first, no matter what.

Still, this man could become very important if he wanted to. Much more important than Jeffrey had ever been. More important than anything, except diving.

"Jean," he whispered, his breath stirring her hair, "do you make love like you dive, so crisp and pure and beautiful?"

She laughed low in her throat, writhing against him in a rhythm that seemed to come naturally to her. "I'm an expert diver," she started, "but not—" The words dissolved in a giggle as he rose over her like a man in a fury.

"Are you going to tell me you don't know how to make love, like you don't know how to dance?" He smiled down at her, sinking both hands into the golden richness of her hair and holding her head before him lovingly. "Do you really expect me to believe that?"

She shook her head, smiling back. That wasn't what she meant at all. But she knew making love with Luke was going to be something fresh and new for her. And she was afraid she wasn't anywhere near to an expert at that. She only hoped she could live up to his expectations, for she knew, unswervingly, they would make love. The sooner the better.

She knew he would lead the way, just as he had at dancing. He would take her up in his arms and carry her to a hidden place, then he would slowly remove her dress and lay her down and . . . .

Something sank away in her and she gasped at the quiver it left behind. She wanted him. She didn't think she'd ever wanted a man before, not like this. But she wanted him with an intensity that hit her with a physical strength.

He was laughing very softly. "We're both going to make love the way you dive," he told her, rubbing his rough cheek against her as lazily as a sleepy cat. "We're going to practice until we get it perfect." He nipped at her love-swollen lips and grinned at her. "Agreed?"

She had no voice left. Everything seemed to sizzle, her skin, her blood, each place where he held her. She could hardly breathe and she was starving for more of his kisses. Instead of answering, she raised her face, parting her lips, begging for more, and he gladly obliged, taking possession of her mouth as though he owned it.

She was beginning to think she really was falling in love with him. She opened herself to his conquest, glad to be his prize.

Maybe this was what she'd been waiting for. She'd always known she would have to start a new life someday, that diving couldn't last forever. She'd avoided thinking about it, because she couldn't imagine anything that could take the place of the sport she loved so completely. She'd never met a man who'd come close to inspiring the kind of passion that could replace it. She hadn't thought such a thing was possible.

And yet in Luke's arms, she began to see that there might be a chance to find happiness. For the first time in her life she saw that there might be hope for her.

His hands skimmed across her body lighting a fire storm wherever they touched. "Come with me, darling," he whispered. "Come to my room and spend the night."

She turned in his arms as he drew her back out onto the terrace. "Look up there." He pointed high above where they stood. "You see that balcony almost at the very top of the tower? That's where I'm staying." His arms came in from behind, his hands cupping her breasts, and she leaned back against him, looking up at the black sky.

"We'll leave open the drapes," he told her softly, "and make love in the starlight. Then in the morning we'll have breakfast on the balcony and watch the sun come up over the desert." He kissed the side of her head. "Tell me you'll come," he murmured.

Jean sighed happily. She'd seldom been so sure of an answer. "I'll come," she replied, closing her eyes and tilting her head back against him. "I'll go anywhere with you."

There was a rustle in the bushes surrounding the terrace. Jean heard the sound and assumed it was some little animal, until she heard the voice that went with it.

"Uncle Luke!"

They both froze, then pulled away from one another as though, Jean realized later when she thought about it, they'd been caught doing something they shouldn't.

She'd known right away that her dream was evaporating. Somehow, just the existence of someone who could call Luke "uncle" in that proprietary way began the job of eating away at her happiness. This was something outside the picture Luke had painted and she knew it would change everything.

He was hastily shoving the ends of his shirt back into his trousers and she wanted to reach out and stop him, as though that would stop the destruction that was going on.

They both peered into the bushes and watched as a young girl emerged, brushing away twigs and talking constantly in a high childish voice. She had a head of long blond hair that glowed in the dark as though it were incandescent, and she moved like an energetic child, but as she came closer, Jean saw she was actually in her teens.

"Uncle Luke, I finally found you! We've been looking all over. Good grief! I've got bush pieces all over me. I may start to sprout."

Luke moved completely away from Jean, leaving her to turn toward the girl. Jean noted the wary look crossing his face and a cold hand began to squeeze her heart. As she watched the girl approach, she felt even worse. She recognized this blond moppet. It was Danni Worth, the diver many considered the main threat to her crown.

"Have you asked her yet?" The girl was beside Luke now, taking his hand affectionately and grinning at Jean in a friendly manner. "We couldn't wait any longer to find out if she'll do it. Of course, I know you said to stay away and leave it to you, but whenever I leave things to you, they turn out different from what I plan, and this has got to be right, or nothing will be gained. So I came—"

"Danni, hold on." Luke looked first annoyed, then reluctantly amused and he reached out to tousle the girl's hair. "I haven't asked her yet, Sugar. You just keep that little mouth buttoned until I do, okay?"

Jean was certain she was the object of their words. This must have something to do with the elusive business proposition Luke had been threatening to offer all night, but neglected to get into, almost as though . . . almost as though he wanted to improve his bargaining position first. She hated herself for thinking that, but she didn't see any alternative.

He was gazing at Jean with a guarded expression. "I think you two know each other?"

Danni's smile looked genuine. Jean tried to match it, but the frost around her heart was beginning to spread and she wasn't sure how well she did.

"We've seen each other at meets over the last year or so," Jean acknowledged.

"You've always been my idol, Jean Archer," Danni told her ingenuously. "Right from the beginning, when I was just a little kid. I've always looked up to you. All us kids do. Why, I had pictures of you on my walls when I was still in a crib."

Jean flashed a look at Luke and found him frowning, as though he knew this meeting was not destined to be the most successful of his career.

"So many years ago?" she responded with just a touch of irony. "I'm flattered." She twisted her hands together in quiet desperation, trying to maintain control.

"You're the best," Danni said with such simple admiration that Jean regretted her impulse toward sarcasm. "You've always represented my main goal."

The girl was even prettier here in the moonlight,

dressed in her white organdy party dress, than she was
in her orange swimsuit, sleek from the water. Jean knew
she was seventeen; at the moment she looked no older
than twelve.

"I'll get mama," she told Luke, spinning away.

"Where did you leave her, in the parking lot?" he
called after her, running a hand through his thick hair.

Danni laughed. "I told you we've been looking everywhere. We were checking to see if your car was here. It
isn't, by the way." She disappeared into the shadows.
"We'll be back in a minute."

Jean wanted to leave very badly. "Luke," she began,
turning toward him.

"No." He read her mind. "No, stay and meet Sheila."
His hand was on her arm as though he feared she'd run
away if he didn't hold her near. "Come sit down. They'll
be here soon."

She followed his lead, almost numb with dread. Just
moments before she'd been floating in a dreamworld of
stars and moonbeams. Now she'd crashed back down to
earth with a jarring thump, and she was sure she wasn't
going to like where she'd landed.

She sat beside Luke and neither spoke. She wanted to
ask him about the proposition, but she couldn't. Whenever she thought about it, a wall of hard clear glass
seemed to crystallize between them. She didn't have the
strength to penetrate it and she was frightened of
trying.

"Is Sheila Danni's mother?" she asked instead, her
voice ringing with a hollow sound against the cold flagstones of the terrace.

"Yes."

There was a pause and then she felt him moving toward her. He was going to explain; she could sense it
and she turned to meet him halfway, anxious that his

explanation would clear away the fear and take them back to where they'd been such a short time before.

"Jean." He touched her shoulder lightly with his fingertips. "Jean, I wish I'd told you—"

"Told me what?" She wasn't sure she really wanted to know. Maybe it would be better to run off into the moonlight and never see Luke again. At least she'd always have the memory of this perfect night. Perfect— until Danni Worth had arrived on the scene.

He glanced toward the bushes as though unsure whether he would be able to get his explanation out without being interrupted.

"I didn't know Danni Worth was your niece," Jean said quickly. "Why didn't you tell me?"

He looked back at her and drummed his fingertips restlessly on the metal tabletop. "She's not my niece," he said evenly. "Not really. Her father was my best friend and she's always called me 'uncle.'"

"Was?" Jean couldn't seem to stop twisting her fingers together. "What happened?"

His handsome face darkened as he frowned. "He died last year after a long bout with cancer," he said, speaking quickly as though the subject still cut deep and he wanted to get it over with as rapidly as possible. "Brock left his wife and daughter in my care and I'm doing the best I can for them."

"Oh." Jean's mouth formed the word but she made no sound. Wife and daughter. It sounded a heavy load. She wondered what Danni's mother was like.

"Here they are!"

As though on cue, Danni came crashing through the greenery dragging an older version of herself behind her.

"Danni, wait! There must be a path. These bushes are scratching me!" The older woman stopped to pull a twig from her dress.

Danni spun to a stop before them like an excited elf, ignoring her mother's complaints. "I told you I'd found them. I don't know why they're hiding out here, but that's okay. We'll join them." She plopped down in a chair across from Luke. "Does the waitress come out here? I'm dying for a soda. Hunting down lost uncles is thirsty work."

Luke rose without answering Danni, welcoming her mother with a warm smile. "Hello, Sheila. I'd like you to meet Jean Archer."

"Jean, I'm so glad to meet you."

The small hand that took Jean's was soft and fragile. Sheila had a sweet southern accent that emphasized her pretty femininity. Her age must have been in the late thirties, but she had a childlike quality that made her look younger. Her blond hair curled around her face in gentle waves and her cotton dress clung to her generous curves.

"I've watched you dive so often," she told Jean. "You're a marvelous champion, a credit to this country's diving program."

She sounded genuine enough. Jean was ashamed of her own feelings, but she couldn't help it. She saw the way the woman looked at Luke, the way he smiled at her. Sheila Worth was one of those small gentle women whom men loved to protect, whether they needed it or not. Surely Luke wasn't finding the role as her guardian as much of a burden as she'd surmised.

"I'll get us something to drink," Luke said quickly, spinning on his heel and leaving them to retreat to the bar.

Jean had the impression he was relieved to escape, but she didn't have time to think about it. Sheila was talking, complimenting her again on her diving, complaining about the twigs that still clung to her clothes from her rush through the bushes, commenting on her dress.

"Aren't you getting cool out here?" she asked, looking the part of an anxious mother. "That's one thing that's so marvelous about the desert. Even if the day is hot, the evening usually cools everything off."

Jean couldn't have told anyone what the temperature was like at the moment. She felt hot one second, cold the next. She wished she were anywhere but here, talking with Danni's mother.

Luke returned with drinks and she wanted to turn to him for refuge, but then she remembered he was the one she really needed shelter from. She was feeling very confused and very much out of place.

"Here we are." Luke placed a tray on the table with three mixed drinks for the adults and a soda for Danni. "I hope you both like old-fashioneds."

Jean wrapped her hands around the frosty glass as though it would save her from drowning. There had to be some way for her to get out of here gracefully. She wanted to get somewhere far away from Luke so she could look at what had happened here in a rational light, unclouded by the emotion she felt in his sphere.

"Danni tells me you haven't yet broached the subject with Jean," Sheila said chidingly to Luke. "Would you like me to ask her myself?"

"No," he said quickly, not looking at Jean. "Why don't you let me talk to her a bit later."

"Why, Luke?" Jean was as surprised as anyone to realize it was her own brittle voice sounding in her ears. "Let's get this out in the open. You've been hinting around about some mysterious 'business proposition' all evening and I must admit, I'm curious."

"You see?" Sheila's laugh was triumphant. "She's ready."

Ready, as though she needed softening up first. So that was it. "Of course, I'm ready." The smile she managed seemed to stretch the skin of her face unbearably. "What is this all about?" She looked straight into Luke's face.

For the first time since she'd met him, she found Luke looking uneasy. His usual air of confident humor was gone. He really didn't want to tell her about this business thing at all. Not yet. Didn't he think she was softened up enough?

"Oh, golly, I'll tell her if no one else will," Danni cried, swinging around in her chair. "We want you to be my new coach. Gary Chapin, the coach I have now, has been great, but he's not quite world caliber, and he admits it himself. He told us you'd be the best person to teach me what I need to know to win a world championship. And Luke will pay you loads and loads of money. So will you do it?" She jumped out of her chair and came over to take Jean's hands and grin down at her, her blue eyes dancing. "I know we'll get on great together. I'm good most of the time, really I am." She tossed Luke a sassy smile. "Aren't I, Uncle Luke?"

Jean was calm and cool. Later she would marvel at how placid she remained as she smiled at the girl. "I haven't retired yet," she reminded her with false cheerfulness. "I'm not looking for a coaching job."

Everyone seemed to be talking at once and her head was aching with the effort of sorting out who was saying what. For just a moment Jean retreated into herself, ignoring them all.

A coaching job. That was what this had all been about, this following her through the parking lot and pretending to hurt his knee—for she'd decided that was exactly what he'd done—and taking her to dinner and dancing with her and kissing her. No, she mustn't think of that. Somehow she would get through the next few minutes without betraying how much that hurt, and then she would make her escape. She swallowed hard and tried to return to what Sheila was saying.

". . . after all, you're well beyond the age most divers keep competing, and I'm sure once you weigh the benefits of a job like this with competing in another World Games, you'll come to the only intelligent conclusion and decide. . . ."

Did they really think she was all washed up and they were doing her a favor by offering her a job? Jean's natural competitive instincts couldn't accept that. No. They wanted to get her out of the way so Danni would be sure to win. That had to be it.

"I'll never keep it up as long as you have," Danni interrupted, shaking her head as though in awe of Jean's age. "All I want is one world championship, and then I want to go to college and be just like everyone else my age." She sat back down and stretched like a furry kitten. "Maybe try a career in show business," she said slyly, glancing at her mother.

"Show business!" Sheila replied with a hint of contempt in her voice. "No daughter of mine is going to make her living that way, I'll tell you." It was obvious this was a running tug-of-war between the two of them.

"Just you wait." Danni flipped back her long silver hair. "When I can sing as well as I dive, you'll be so proud. I'll be on television and everything."

Jean knew, suddenly, that Danni went after everything with the fierce intensity she showed on the diving platform. That was fine. She didn't mind stiff competition.

But she did mind being considered a has-been before she was ready to admit defeat. She did mind being used. There was a hollow sick feeling inside where just a short time before she'd been feeling the excitement of a woman falling in love.

"I wish you luck, Danni," she said, still smiling her artificial smile. "I'm sure you'll do well at whatever you decide to go for. But I'm not a coach and I don't intend to be." She took a long sip of her drink, hardly aware of what it was, trying to think of a way to leave gracefully.

"But what are you going to do?" Danni seemed genuinely interested. "I mean, you're too old to go on with diving much longer. What will you do if you don't coach?"

"Jean is studying to be a physical therapist," Luke replied before she had a chance to answer. "I'm sure she'll carve out a successful career in that, if that's what she decides to do."

He was answering for her again. She felt her back rise, just as it had when he'd tried to help her out with the reporters. She didn't need protection. She could take care of herself.

"I'm going to dive, Danni," she said quietly. "I'm going to dive for another ten years."

There. It was out. She'd never actually said it aloud before, but she'd been thinking it for months. She took another long drink before she could look the others in the eye, conscious of the awkward silence as they stared at her.

"That's...that's just impossible," Danni said at last, shaking her head. "No one has ever done it. You'll never make it."

Jean lifted her head high. "I'll make it," she promised, as much to herself as to the girl. "Now if you'll excuse me, I must go home. I'm in training." She stood. "See you at the World Games, Danni," she said firmly. "Nice to have met you all."

Sheila rose to stop her with a hand on her arm. "I

think we rather surprised you with this," she said kindly, her wide blue eyes as earnest as her daughter's. "Please think it over. We'll talk again."

Not if Jean could help it. How she prayed they were all leaving Las Vegas very soon. She took a step and stopped to collect herself before going on. The terrace seemed to spin for a moment but she kept her balance. "Goodbye," she said lightly.

Turning, she fled back into the crowded disco. The noise hit her like a wall of sound as she entered, throwing her head back and shooting adrenaline through her senses. The place was full now and she had to push her way through the bobbing forms. As the lights flashed and ricocheted around her, she felt as though she'd entered a nightmare world. But at least she'd escaped the awful scene on the terrace.

She might have known she couldn't get away that easily. As she made her way blindly through the surging dancers and stabbing lights, Luke appeared at her shoulder, putting a protective arm around her waist and pushing aside people with the other hand.

"You don't have to help me," she told him, almost shouting to compete with the loud music that rocked the room. "In fact, I'd rather you didn't."

"You'd rather I go to hell," he said agreeably, pulling her more tightly to him and opening the final barrier so that they could both escape into the hallway. "But I won't. I'm going to stay around and bother you instead."

"Please leave me alone," she insisted, trying to walk very quickly to get away from him, but tripping on the thick carpet and landing solidly in his arms. "I don't want to have anything to do with you," she cried, pulling away and lunging toward the lobby.

His hand hooked into the crook of her arm and she

found herself snapping back toward him like the end of a rubber band. Was she ever going to get out of here?

"Let me go," she hissed furiously, trying to work his fingers loose. "You've done enough damage for one day."

"Damage?" He spun her around so that he held her squarely in his embrace, heedless of the flow of the crowd around them. "How have I damaged you, Jean?"

No, he must never know how close she'd come!

Holding her hands stiffly against his wide chest, she glared into his blue eyes. "You've made me break training, that's how. I'm supposed to be in bed by ten and I know it's way past that now."

"Cinderella," he murmured, a smile twisting his lips. "Is your world going to fall apart if you don't get home by midnight?"

It's already fallen apart, thanks to you, she thought, pressing her lips together "My taxi just might turn into a pumpkin if I don't get out there," she said to make him think she was going along with his joke.

"Let it," he answered, his gaze on her lips. "You could always take refuge here with me. I don't turn into a pumpkin at all."

The gall of the man! After all he'd done, he still hoped to talk her into spending the night with him.

She forced a bit more space between them, under the ruse of wanting to look more fully into his face. "What do you turn into, Luke?" she asked. "What does lie on the other side of your good-humored tyranny?"

Far from taking offense at her jab, he grinned. "Come on up to my room with me and I'll show you," he said huskily. "Remember the starlight on the sheets and breakfast on the balcony I promised you?"

Fury surged through her in a hot wave. Did he think she was so overwhelmed by his compelling sexuality that she would trot happily behind him like a puppy dog? He could think again.

"Take your hands off me, Luke Chisholm, or I'm going to cause a big scene right here in the lobby of the hotel where you're staying. I don't think you really want that."

Something in the way she spit out the words through clenched teeth seemed finally to communicate to him just how angry she was, for he slowly released her, searching the depths of her gaze for some further sign of what she was feeling.

"I'll drive you home," was all he said as they began to walk quickly down the corridor again.

"Don't bother," she replied. "I'd rather take a cab." She slid a sidelong glance his way. "Besides, I think you left your car somewhere today, didn't you?"

He nodded, returning her glance. "That's right, I did. Okay, I'll ride with you in the cab."

"That won't be necessary." She swept through the glass door being held open for her and walked quickly to the closest taxi.

"It may not be necessary," he agreed, right behind her, "but I'm going to do it anyway."

He was inside the cab before she had a chance to stop him, so she merely glared at him again, then leaned forward to tell the driver where to take her.

The cab started off with a lurch that sent her back against the seat, and Luke was there to take her hand in his.

"Jean, I want to explain about what happened—"

"Explain?" Her laugh tinkled like broken crystal. "I don't think you need to explain at all. You told me from the beginning you had a business proposition to make to me. I only wish you'd broached it right away. It would've saved us both a lot of time."

He laced his long fingers through hers. "You would've turned me down flat."

She stared out at the shimmering Las Vegas night, the colored lights turning midnight as bright as a desert at noon. "I would've turned you down flat," she agreed, trying to ignore the warmth of his hand on hers. "But what's the difference? I'm doing that anyway."

"No, you're not."

She swung around to look at him. "Yes, I am. You just haven't realized it yet." She tried to pull her hand from his, but he held on more tightly.

"No. You can turn down Danni. You can turn down Sheila. But I haven't even made *my* sales pitch to you yet. You can't turn me down until I do."

His arm was around her and she was sliding up against him, coming into contact with the excitement of his hard body once again.

"Is this what your sales pitch consists of?" she asked shakily, wishing she was being a little more forceful about pushing him away but unable to gather the will for it.

"Not really." His voice was as soft as a leopard's fur. "I call this laying the groundwork."

She let him kiss her, thinking to merely endure it and show him how little he moved her, but she found herself kissing him back almost immediately. His golden touch was too seductive and she took him in as though she was starving for his brand of love.

"How many times have I kissed you now?" he whispered against her neck. "Five times? Six? And each time it's better." He nipped at the tender skin behind her ear. "But there's an odd aftereffect." He raised his head to smile down at her. "No matter how satisfying your kisses are, they only make me hungrier for more."

He leaned down to kiss her again, but finally she

pulled together enough strength to fend him off. Turning sharply, she avoided his mouth, pushing hard against him.

"You're going to have to learn to control your appetite," she admonished as she forced him away. "And next time you get 'the munchies,' go chew on someone else!"

The cab pulled up in front of her apartment and she flung herself out of the door. If she could just get in her front door without letting him touch her again, she might be safe. But one more kiss and she knew she would be putty in his hands.

Luke emerged from the cab and stood looking at her. She backed quickly toward her door, fumbling in her bag for her keys.

"I'm going to leave you to pay the driver," she called back to him. "I'm sure you can find some spare change out of all that 'loads and loads' of money you were going to pay me to coach Danni."

"We've still got to talk." He was walking toward her and she panicked, groping wildly for the keys that seemed to be purposely eluding her. Somehow she knew she would never make it in her doorway alone if he reached her before she got the lock open. And once he was inside . . . .

"You can talk," she called to him, backing against her locked door. "But I don't have any listening left."

Her fingers closed around the cold metal of her key ring and she pulled it triumphantly from her bag. "So save your breath." She turned the key in the lock and stepped inside. "Thank you for a very mixed evening," she said quickly. "Goodbye."

Once inside she collapsed, all her brave energy spent. She sank back against the closed door breathing heavily, as though she'd just run a wild race across the sand.

Then she held her breath, listening. There wasn't a sound. He was still out there, standing in front of her apartment, waiting. What would she do if he knocked? Suddenly she knew. She would let him in. She had only so much strength and she'd used it all up.

When she heard the taxi's engine start up again, she let the air out with a long trembling sigh. He was gone, maybe forever. Oh yes, it had better be forever. But he left behind him a very changed woman.

5

"Higher, higher. You need a lot more lift."

Jean sighed, readjusting the harness that held her to the apparatus above the blue trampoline. Eleanor, the coach she more usually referred to as her slave driver, was cracking her whip with special fury today. Following orders, Jean jumped higher, tucking and turning in the air.

"That was better," Eleanor called. "But try to get a little more arch in the pullout."

They used the trampoline to help develop newer, more difficult moves for Jean to incorporate into her diving repertoire. In the harness, she could leap high in the air, twisting and flipping, and know she was safe from injury. This way, she could get a new movement down perfectly before actually using it in a dive.

"Let's call it a morning," Eleanor said after Jean had tried the move a few more times. "It's almost time for your ten-thirty class, and I've got to call Mike."

Jean bounced to the edge of the trampoline and jumped down to where her coach could help her unwind from the harness.

Eleanor was small and dark with hair cut short in an elfin cap about her head. Her quick graceful way of moving often reminded Jean of a hummingbird. She was the same counselor who had introduced Jean to diving at camp so many years ago. Now that Jean's parents and Uncle Max had died, leaving her the trust fund that took care of her living expenses, Eleanor was just about the closest thing to family she had left.

"How is Mike?" she asked casually as they worked on the ties. "I haven't seen him for a long time."

It was true, she realized. Mike used to hang around all the time. He and Eleanor had been married a little over a year ago, and lately he'd been pretty much absent from the workouts.

"He's fine," Eleanor answered shortly. "Busy."

Mike had recently opened his own landscaping company. "I guess busy is good when you work for yourself," Jean said musingly. "But I miss him. Why don't the two of you come over for dinner some night this week?" There'd been a time when they'd gotten together weekly for a big pot of spaghetti.

To her surprise, Eleanor seemed to be avoiding her eyes. "Oh, I don't know. It's the end of the month and I think we'll be spending our evenings working on the books," she said evasively. "If you can put the rest of this stuff away, I'm going to run and give him a call. I promised to get some information for him and he needs it right away."

Jean nodded, but she stood watching her friend walk out of the swimming stadium. Now that she thought about it, Eleanor had been acting strangely for quite some time. She hadn't paid a lot of attention, thinking it was a passing mood that Eleanor would get over soon enough. But it seemed to be getting worse, not better.

Jean frowned thoughtfully. She hoped there was nothing wrong between the newlyweds. She would have to remember to ask Eleanor if there was anything she could do to help.

But right now it was time to get ready for class. She walked quickly to the locker room and opened her own cubby hole to pull out the brown slacks and pink cotton sweater she wanted to wear on campus. Stashing away her gym clothes, she put on her street wear, bundled her books together and dashed out the locker-room door.

All in all, she was doing quite well. She'd started out her day at dawn swimming a series of brisk laps, then went through her dives before doing the trampoline work. Other than a slight grogginess at first because she hadn't had enough sleep the night before, she hadn't noticed any problems. Maybe Luke Chisholm hadn't altered her life so much, after all.

She swung along the walkway to the Medical Center with long easy strides, letting her hair fly in the warm breeze. Nothing had really changed. If anything, her determination to retain her championship was even stronger now than it had been before. She was going to spend every waking moment between now and the games in July with that goal in mind.

She slipped into class only a few minutes late. The professor had barely begun his lecture on tendonitis. She pulled out her notebook and scribbled quick notes, jotting down every third word he said but not really hearing him.

Yes, she told herself, it was going to be easy to forget Luke Chisholm. She might have to work on it a bit, but that would be no problem. She'd worked on tougher things before.

She got busy on it right away and managed to completely erase him from her mind for all of three minutes during the next hour.

This forgetting business was going to take concentration, she admitted to herself as she walked back to the stadium after class. Right now the man was very fresh in her mind. She could feel the imprint of his lips on hers, the sense of excitement his hard body stirred in her.

Those images would begin to fade soon and then she'd be in better shape.

She met Bette at the quad where the cement paths crossed.

"Hi there. Going my way?"

Bette grinned, her round face open and welcoming. "Sure am. And I'm bringing lunch if you don't have any other plans." She held up a brown paper bag.

"Great." the two of them fell into step beside one another. "How about a picnic in the grass?"

They walked around behind the stadium and settled on a green area between the building and the tennis courts, where they could hear the splashing from the pool and watch the tennis balls zip back and forth. The day was warm and lazy and the setting seemed a hundred miles away from the fast-paced life on the Las Vegas strip, even though it was just a few blocks away.

"What's the matter?" Bette asked as they unwrapped their submarine sandwiches.

"Nothing's the matter," Jean answered a bit defensively.

Bette cocked her head to the side, holding up a hand to shade her eyes. "You look different somehow."

"I do not!" There was something very threatening to her peace of mind in that assessment.

"Well, pardon me," Bette answered with sardonic humor. "It must be the sun in my eyes. It's baking my brain."

Jean laughed and reached out to touch her friend's hand. "I'm sorry I snapped at you." She bit her lip, wondering if she should tell Bette all about what had happened, the night before. It would do her good to get it off her chest, but at the same time, running through it again would only make her remember it more clearly.

Bette took a bite of her giant sandwich, struggling to

get it all in her mouth, then chewed while staring at Jean thoughtfully. "What happened when that Luke Chisholm character got hold of you?" she asked with penetrating perception.

Jean stared down at her uneaten meal, then looked up with a rueful grin. "Oh Bette, he really put me through the wringer," she wailed.

"I knew it." Bette set down her sandwich with a thump and turned all her attention on Jean. "I could sense it the moment I laid eyes on that guy. Tell me all about it."

"He . . . Jeffrey and I had a date so he ended up taking us both out to dinner at the Camelot, but Jeffrey got called to the hospital so he and I . . . ."

"Yes?" Bette prompted eagerly.

"We . . . we went dancing and . . . Bette, he was so easy to be with. He did everything so well, as though it were all second nature to him, and he made me feel . . . pretty."

Bette sighed. "You are pretty, Jean. You're the only one who doesn't know that."

Jean shook her head impatiently. "This was different. He made me feel special, like I meant something to him. I . . . ." She found herself carefully rewrapping her sandwich in the cellophane, even though she hadn't eaten a bite. "I thought," she whispered very softly, "that I was falling in love."

"Oh, Jean!" Bette seemed about to jump up and dance a jig. "That's wonderful!"

"No." Jean shook her head slowly. "It's not at all wonderful." She raised her face to look into her friend's eyes. "You see, it was all an act. He's Danni Worth's guardian and he was buttering me up, trying to get me to retire so she can win the championship at the World Games in July. He offered me a job as her coach. Can you imagine?" The anger flooded her again. "I mean, who do they think they're kidding?"

"Oh, honey." Bette reached toward her in helpless sympathy. "You turned him down, didn't you?"

She nodded.

"Then it's all over. Don't think about it anymore."

Jean nodded again, toying with her wrapped submarine. "That's just what I plan to do."

There was a long silence. The sound of tennis balls plopping mixed with the buzzing of a few wayward insects.

"Are you going out with Luke Chisholm again?" Bette asked hopefully, as though she'd been bottling up the question and couldn't hold it back any longer.

"Bette!" Jean said indignantly. "Of course not."

She sighed. "He is such a good-looking man," she said regretfully.

"He is a phony," Jean said emphatically. "And I never want to see him again."

Bette threw her a glance that held worry mixed with doubt. "Okay. Eat your food and I promise not to mention him."

Jean slowly unwrapped her sandwich again and forced down a bite or two while the two of them chatted about inconsequential items, steering carefully clear of the subject of Luke Chisholm. Finally, as they gathered together the remnants of their picnic, Bette got down to the reason she'd come.

"I've got a problem, Jean, and I'm hoping you can help me with it."

Jean turned toward her friend in surprise. Bette was the sort of woman who was always there for others. She very seldom asked for anything for herself. Jean hoped she'd be able to help her with whatever was bothering her.

"What is it? I'll do anything I can."

She could see by the cloudy expression in her friend's eyes that this was much more serious than she was saying.

"Oh, it's nothing really." Bette waved away her look of concern as she bent to pick up a stray bit of paper in the grass. "It's just that...I took Andy in for his weekly checkup yesterday and the surgeon seems to feel he isn't responding to treatment as he should. He can't seem to get up on his legs again, and the pain...." Her voice faded into something suspiciously like a sob.

Bette's twelve-year-old son had taken a bad fall from a horse two months before. He'd fractured his right hipbone. The break itself wasn't unusual or particularly dangerous, but Jean knew how hard it had been to keep him down at first. He'd wanted to act like a normal boy, even without being able to use his legs as a normal boy could. He'd been ecstatic when he'd been allowed up on crutches. By now, he should have been well on the road to recovery.

"Bette." Jean put a hand on her arm. "What is it? How can I help?"

Bette's smile was watery. "He can get around on crutches, but it's so painful he won't make the attempt to get beyond that. And, of course, the longer he delays, the harder it is for his body to respond. And if he's to regain normal use of his legs...." She took a deep breath. "All I want is a little advice. The surgeon thinks Andy could be helped by daily sessions of physical therapy. From what he said, I gather it will have to be an extensive program." Bette sighed. "Do you know anyone good? Oh Jean, I hate to just pick a name out of the phone book. The surgeon had to look up names himself. He didn't seem to have anyone he'd worked with before to recommend. You're my only hope. Do you know someone you really trust?"

Jean threw her arms around her friend and gave her a quick hug. "Of course, I do. I know plenty of good therapists and I'll go with you, if you like, to pick one out."

"Would you?" Her round face looked brighter already. "I'd be so relieved. Jean, you don't know how this has tortured me. It's so important to choose the right person, someone who will be able to motivate Andy to try. The doctor warned me that his tendons could start to deteriorate if something isn't begun soon. And once they get beyond a certain point...."

Her voice broke and Jean hugged her more tightly. She wished with sudden passion that she were a licensed therapist herself. How she would like to be able to help Bette in a more direct way! But she wasn't licensed, and anyway, with the amount of work she was going to have to put in on her diving for the next few months, there would be no time to set up an extensive program of physical therapy for Andy. But she would certainly do what she could.

She and Bette made a date to get together the next morning to start therapist-shopping and she said goodbye to her friend and walked slowly back to the swimming stadium. She couldn't help but think about Andy's cute little freckled face. She remembered how he'd bragged about his riding the last time she'd seen him before the accident.

"Well, if I don't decide to be a cowboy in Wyoming, I might try rodeo riding for a while," he'd told her seriously, pushing his ever-present cowboy hat to the back of his head. "Uh course, I still might be a fireman during the summer."

Jean smiled as she thought of his shining green eyes,

so full of plans for the future. It was a future that would be considerably less promising if his pelvis didn't heal properly, and he didn't regain the full use of his legs.

He was a darling boy. Bette had raised him on her own for the last ten years, ever since he was two, and she'd done a darn good job of it.

Bette had come to Las Vegas as a girl right out of high school, looking for a job in the chorus of one of the big shows. She'd never landed that, but she had a quick mind and good hand-eye coordination, and she'd taken the two week course for dealers at one of the downtown hotels. Soon she was dealing blackjack on a green felt table.

She'd met Will there. Will was a gambler, but unlike Jean's Uncle Max, Will lost more than he won. He didn't travel the professional circuit. He tried his luck, and each new "infallible" system, on the tables at the clubs downtown or at the hotels on the Strip, whenever he had enough to hold his own. When he was winning he was the most generous man in the world. It had been on a long winning streak that he'd met and married Bette.

The winning streak had soon faded, and each year the wins got fewer and the losses piled higher. Bette had a two-year-old son before she finally admitted to herself she was married to a compulsive gambler. When Will decided to move on and try his luck in Reno, Bette stayed behind.

She'd worked at the university administration office ever since. Though the pay was lower than what she could make dealing, she hated gambling, the clubs, and all that went with that life-style. She'd seen the underside of the glitter and she wouldn't touch that sort of thing again.

She'd worked so hard to make a good life for her son. Jean hoped the therapist would be just what Andy needed.

She grinned as she realized how much time she'd just spent thinking about something other than the man who'd disrupted her life. Good. It was working.

She put on her blue bathing suit and spent some time in meditation on her mat before going out to resume practice.

The stadium was a huge open-ceilinged affair with a diving pool at one end and a swimming pool at the other. Rows of bleachers lined every side.

Jean generally had the diving pool pretty much to herself. The university diving team practiced in the evenings. The swimming team was another matter. There were members of the swim team practicing at all hours of the day.

Eleanor was in a better mood for the afternoon session. "Is everything okay with you and Mike?" Jean asked when they met at the diving platform.

"Sure." Eleanor smiled her quick flashing smile. "We had a fight this morning, that's all. I called him and everything's fine now."

"I'm glad."

Jean began to run through her required dives, beginning with the front dives, then going into her back dive layout. She was standing, toes gripping the edge of the board, arms straight out before her, when a movement along the side of the pool broke her concentration. She'd already begun her spring; it was too late to stop. She did the best she could to save it, but her mind was on the interloper.

She knew it was Luke. She'd been waiting for him all day, but she hadn't known it until now. Pulling herself back out of the water, she refused to look toward where he was. She could tell he'd stopped in the bleacher area along the side of the pool, but she forced herself not to glance his way. Instead, she climbed up on the board again and walked out to the end.

"That was really terrible," Eleanor called up to her. "What happened anyway?"

Jean shook her head and went into her stance again. She wasn't going to let him shake her. Gritting her teeth, she did the same dive again. This time she nailed it.

She went on for almost an hour, dive after dive, with Eleanor calling a comment or suggestion now and then. Finally, as she was climbing out of the water after a particularly difficult somersault tuck, Eleanor came up to her before she reached the board.

"There's a man whose been watching you from the bleachers for a long time," she told her, peering around her to look at Luke. "Anyone you know?"

For the first time, Jean swung around and glared right at him, her hands on her hips. "Yes, I know him," she said loudly. "He's Danni Worth's guardian. He must be here to spy on us."

Eleanor's jaw dropped in disbelief. "Well, I never! The nerve of some people!" Her tiny hands balled into fists. "I'm going to give that man a piece of my mind!"

Jean watched in amusement as the small woman marched across the deck toward where Luke was sitting. He was stretched back, his feet up on the bench in front of him, his elbows resting on the bench behind, his mouth relaxed in a lazy smile.

You won't be smiling long, Luke Chisholm, Jean thought to herself. Eleanor was small but she had a big temper. As she confronted Luke, she looked like a bantam hen guarding her barnyard from a marauding mountain lion. Jean flipped her wet hair behind her and stepped up on the board. There was no need to watch the carnage. She already knew who was going to win this encounter. She might as well get on with her practice.

When she climbed out of the pool they were still talking. She tried a one-and-a-half somersault tuck, then a pike, then both dives again, and still they were talking. In fact, as she glanced toward them while pulling out of the pool, they were both facing her way. They were talking about her.

She climbed the metal ladder to the board and walked out slowly, steadying herself. If they were going to talk about her, she'd give them something to talk about. She prepared to do a reverse one-and-a-half with two-and-a-half twists, the dive she often used as a showstopper in meets. Taking two deep, cleansing breaths, she set her mental attitude.

It wasn't working. A sudden finger of panic slivered through her. She was nervous, more nervous than she usually was before a crowd of thousands. Her concentration was gone. She would have to think of some way to get it back quickly.

She touched the medallion on the gold chain around her neck. It was a small golden playing card made to look like an ace of diamonds. Uncle Max had given it to her to bring her luck in diving and it always had. But right now she needed more than luck.

Walking back across the board, she shook out her muscles, trying to relax. In her mind she made the dive, visualizing every step as though she were seeing it on an internal television screen, ending with the final plunge.

See, she told herself. *See, it's easy. I've done it before. I can do it again.*

Okay. She was ready now. Confidently she stepped out to the end of the board.

One jump and she was in the air, twisting and turning, then straight as a silver wing, every muscle rigid, cutting through the water with barely a ripple. She'd done a perfect dive and she knew it.

"Row of tens for that one, Jean." Eleanor met her at

the stairs as she came out of the water. "Best you've ever done. Do it like that at the World Games and you'll knock 'em on their cans."

Jean glanced quickly at the bleachers. Luke was still there.

"I thought you were going to show him the way to go home," she said lightly, looking questioningly at Eleanor.

"Hey, that guy is something else." Eleanor shrugged. "He knows what he's talking about. He told me to watch out for the way you kind of tuck your head right at entry. I watched and darned if he wasn't right on. I'd never noticed that. We're going to have to work on it."

"Eleanor! The man is Danni Worth's guardian."

"I know. Maybe that's where he comes by all this know-how." She snuck a look back at him. "And he's cuter than heck, too, don't you think? Come on, Jean. We've only got another half hour and I want you to work on that tuck of the head at entry. Clearing that up might just help us with that problem you've had on the reverse pike."

Jean sighed and climbed up on the board. After all, what more could he do to her? She'd already proved she could do her best with him watching. She would just forget he was there.

That worked just fine while she was diving, but the time came to end the practice and Eleanor left her alone to walk back to the locker room. She had to pass right in front of Luke. Steeling herself, she determined to walk by without a word.

"Not even a smile?" He sprang up from the bench as she passed and fell in step with her. "Not even a soft curse for old times' sake?"

She looked at the ground, uncomfortably aware of how vulnerable she was in her thin one-piece swimming suit, with her hair wet and her arms and legs bare. Gooseflesh prickled across her skin as tiny drops of water sped down her spine. Hugging her towel to her chest, she walked on without answering him.

"Are we going to play this game again?" he asked. When she didn't answer, he took her wrist in his hand and pulled her to a halt.

"Am I going to have to guess which exit you're going to try to escape through?"

Finally, she raised her face to his. "Why don't you leave me alone, Luke?" she asked, trying to keep a tremor out of her voice.

He smiled suddenly, reaching down to tap her long water-laden eyelashes with a gentle touch. "You look like you've got diamonds all around your eyes," he said softly, letting his finger lower to trace the line of a drop of water as it shimmered down her cheek. "A water princess."

She felt as though her insides were melting. He was dressed in a black lightweight turtleneck sweater in a soft wool blend and gray slacks that fit snugly on his muscular legs. She wanted to feel his arms around her as she'd felt them the night before. If she wasn't careful she would reach for him automatically without letting her defense system take over.

"Luke, please leave me alone," she said again, almost begging.

"No." Suddenly his voice was harsh and his eyes had hardened. "No, I'm not going to leave you alone. I want a chance to explain and you're going to give it to me."

She shook her head, miserable. "Nothing you say can change anything. Save us both a lot of—" she was about to say heartbreak, but she quickly bit it back "—wasted effort. We've got other things to do."

"I'm going to make you understand."

As if she didn't already understand perfectly well. "Not here." She pulled out of his grasp and back toward the locker-room door. "Not now."

"Then when, Jean?" He came toward her as though he would follow her right into her sanctuary. "Where? You name the time and place."

"No." She shook her head. "Just go away, Luke. Leave me in peace." She backed through the swinging doors and hurried into the showers, bent on washing away the lingering pain of this encounter.

Turning on the water as hot and hard as she could stand it, she peeled off her swimsuit and stood beneath the steamy stinging spray, closing her eyes and letting it cleanse her mind along with her body.

How long would it take before Luke would give up and go home? She had no way of knowing, but she spent longer in the shower than she ever had before in her life, and then ate up another hour drying her hair and dressing in the pink sweater and chocolate-brown slacks. By the time she was ready to go there was no one left in the locker room. For all she knew, there was no one left on the whole campus.

She wouldn't go out the emergency exit this time. She had nothing to hide and he had no right to complicate her life. She walked out into the pool area, head high and determined. Luke was nowhere to be seen.

She went out through the main exit and headed for the parking lot. Her car was waiting where she'd parked it and it was empty. She got in, still looking around as though she expected to see Luke appear from behind another parked car at any moment. But there was nothing. A curious lump sat on top of the sense of relief in her chest, holding it down so that she could take little joy in it. Maybe he really had given up.

She drove home slowly, winding through the quiet

residential streets with a mysterious reluctance she couldn't analyze. When she pulled up in front of her apartment, she finally knew what it was.

He was standing in front of her place, leaning against the front-door frame, waiting for her. She turned off the engine and sat looking down the street for a long moment, then turned to look at him.

He didn't move. With a sigh of total resignation, she opened the car door, stepped out and walked slowly up to meet him.

"What would you have done if I hadn't come home?" she asked when she got within speaking distance.

He shrugged nonchalantly. "You'd have to come home sometime."

He moved aside and she stuck her key in the lock. "I guess you think I'm going to have to let you in, don't you?"

She felt his hand on her hair as she bent to work on the stubborn lock. "Of course, you'll let me in," he said lightly. "Your natural sense of fair play won't allow you to do anything else."

The lock finally clicked free and the door swung open. "You take a lot for granted." She turned to look up into his face. "I really don't think this will serve any purpose."

His eyes were as clear as a mountain stream, his slightly shaggy hair thick and shining in the late-afternoon sunlight. "I just want a chance to explain," he claimed. "Let me in, Jean. You won't regret it."

There really wasn't much choice any longer. She felt as though she'd stepped off the security of the shore onto a raft that was starting a long hurtle down a river of rapids. She saw the danger ahead, but it was too late to turn back now.

"Is that a promise?" she asked softly as he came in behind her, but he didn't expect an answer.

"Sit down." She motioned toward the couch. "Would you like a drink?" She began to move around the room busily, setting down her things and moving papers, picking up an African violet to check its furry leaves.

"No." He was behind her, his hands gently but firmly on her wrists, forcing her to put down the plant. "All I want is a little talking. Come over and sit with me."

She followed him to the couch a bit numbly, sinking down on the cushions beside him with a feeling of dread closing her throat. He was so close, so large, so incredibly attractive. A strand of his hair had fallen over his forehead and she wanted to reach out and rake it back where it belonged, but she didn't dare.

When he reached out to put a hand on her shoulder, she shrugged it away. "No," she said more firmly than she'd thought she could possibly speak to him. "No touching."

He frowned and something flashed behind his steady gaze. It was obvious he didn't much like taking orders of that kind, but he sat back. For now, he would be obedient.

"Everything got turned upside down yesterday," he said by way of prologue. "It was my fault. I started out with a purpose, but I got sidetracked." His mouth softened into a lopsided grin. "I didn't realize you were going to turn out to be quite such a distraction."

"Why don't you get this finished?" She had to be very wary here. If she started taking his compliments seriously she would be in big trouble.

"What's your hurry?" He glanced around the room. "Got another date with Jeffrey?"

She didn't, but that was none of his business. "The explanation?"

He stretched his long legs straight out before him. "Brock Worth was my best friend. We played college ball together, then we were together on the 49ers." His smile turned bittersweet. "We were close in the way men often are. We liked to play a little golf together, bowl, maybe sit around and watch the games on Sunday. But we also had something more. We could really talk to each other, tell each other things we couldn't tell anyone else."

He wasn't looking at her any longer. Instead, he was staring at a staghorn fern on her wall, as though what he was telling her was too personal to tell easily.

"He told me all his dreams, his hopes for his little girl." He threw his head back and looked at her ceiling. "He was so proud of her diving. He knew she had it in her to be the very best. When he found out his illness was terminal . . . ."

He stopped to swallow and Jean felt a rush of sympathy. Involuntarily she reached toward him, but she stopped herself before she connected.

". . . he told me it was up to me. I had to make sure she got every chance. I swore to him that I would do just that. And I mean to."

He looked at her. "Danni is on the verge of greatness. She needs the very best coach we can find to put her over the edge. That's why we came here. You're the best there is."

Her mouth was dry. "I'm flattered. But I'm not a coach."

He cocked an eyebrow. "Was Eleanor a coach when she began training you?"

Jean couldn't resist a smile. "Not really. But the two of us had time to grow together."

He nodded. "We don't have time, do we? That's why we came. I was to go to you, make you an offer you wouldn't refuse and have Danni in your care by this morning." He laughed softly. "As you know, I failed."

Jean took a deep breath. "There are other coaches."

"Oh sure. There are other coaches." He turned more fully toward her. "But I don't want to talk about the coaching right now. I want to talk about you and me."

Her hand went nervously to the chain around her neck. "You and me?" she repeated. "There is no 'you and me.'"

His chuckle was low and he moved closer still. This time when his hand settled on her shoulder, she didn't force it away. "Don't play with me, woman," he said with silky intent. "There's been a 'you and me' since the first. This kind of chemistry doesn't come along every day. You should be rejoicing instead of fighting it."

His arrogant assumption that she should take joy in his interest in her, in her terrifyingly overwhelming reaction to him, grated a bit, but she soon forgot her annoyance as she realized from the new light in his eyes that he was beginning to forget about rational discussion. Physical attraction was fast taking over.

6

"I SAID NO TOUCHING," Jean reminded Luke a bit desperately as his arm slid around her shoulders.

He was so big he seemed to be everywhere. His wide chest blotted out the rest of the room, and his arms could reach around the world. She had no place to run, no place to hide. And she wasn't sure she'd take an escape if one was offered to her.

"But you didn't really mean it," he countered confidently. "Relax, Jean. Let it grow."

Let it grow. But what would it become—a relationship to nurture them both or a monster to be put to a painful death? Jean shuddered and tried to pull away from his increasingly ardent embrace.

"This isn't explaining anything to me," she protested as his warm mouth began a slow exploration of the sensitive line of her throat. "You said you would explain."

"I am explaining," he murmured against her neck. "Believe me, Jean, this explains it all."

She put out her hands to push him away but as they slid across the soft wool of his sweater, a thick languorous lethargy began to sap her strength, draining her will to resist.

"Luke," she moaned as he pressed her more firmly back against the pillows in the corner of the couch. "Luke, you said you wanted to talk."

"I changed my mind." He raised his head and tugged at the collar of her sweater, revealing the base of her neck. With two fingers he slowly covered the pulse that beat there. as though reaching to capture her heart. "Did I do that, Jean?" he whispered, his blue gaze burning with silver heat. "Did I start that pounding in your blood?"

He knew the answer and she didn't bother to express it aloud. Instead, she moaned again, rubbing her hands against the seductive smoothness of his chest, while he bent to kiss the pulse point.

"I'll make it beat faster, Jean," he promised huskily. "I'll set your blood on fire."

"Luke. . . ." She was uttering a protest, but at the same time her hands reached up to his thick rich hair, threading through the wealth of it, pressing his face against her.

"I watched you diving, Jean," he said as he nuzzled into the hollow of her shoulder, pulling open the collar wide enough to find her warm skin. "I watched your beautiful body sail through the air, and I wanted you like I've never wanted any other woman."

Her heart caught in her throat at his words. Could he really mean it? She wanted to believe every nuance.

"I ache for you," he growled, his warm breath searing her skin. "I want you so much it hurts." He pressed down on top of her, holding her a captive of his strong body, letting her feel the fullness of his desire against her.

His hand slipped down to curve around the swell of her breast. The pink wool of her sweater was soft, but as his fingers teased her nipple erect, she became infinitely more sensitive to the texture of it.

"That's it, darling," he crooned near her ear. "Let your body come alive for me. Then you won't need any other explanations."

Explanations? Her mind had gone blank and she

couldn't think what he was talking about. She didn't
want explanations any longer. All she wanted was the
hard smooth heat of him against her. Some protective
shield inside her had been stripped away and the raw
open hunger it revealed was new to her.

His hand was under her sweater now, gliding slowly
over her rib cage, covering her small rounded breast as
though he was devouring it. As his palm scraped across
the hardened tip she drew in her breath with a gasping
shiver and she felt him laugh with delight.

She arched back against the pressure of his hips and
as she did so he yanked her sweater up over her head in
one swift move.

"Oh!" Instinctively she crossed her arms in front of
herself, protecting her naked breasts, but he would have
none of that.

"Let me look at you, water princess," he whispered,
forcing her arms back above her head, holding her
wrists so that he would have no interference. "Let me
look at the pure golden beauty of you."

He held her prisoner with his hips and one hand on
her wrists while the other began a taunting exploration
that promised to drive her wild with longing for fulfill-
ment. Teasingly, he barely touched one nipple, then the
other, laughing softly as the small dusky buds strained
for more of him. He ran his hand down between her
breasts, his fingers massaging with feather-light forays
across her white skin, then circling her navel.

"Luke," she moaned, writhing beneath his hold.

"Not yet, darling," he warned, leaning down to nuz-
zle the soft slope of her breast, then taking one tawny
tip gently between his teeth and tugging on it while his
tongue made its own caress upon the tender surface.

"Luke!" The name came out in a growling command
and she surged from beneath his control, pulling her

hands free and reaching to pull him down to her with tempestuous urgency. She needed him, wanted him, as she'd never known she could want a man. Her mouth opened as his came down on it, matching him thrust for thrust, and her hands pushed beyond the barrier of his belt, finding their way to the hard solid muscles of his buttocks.

"Oh, Luke," she said again, her fingernails digging in with quick need. *Love me now,* she wanted to cry out. *Love me now, I need you so.* Could he hear her plea in the air that quivered between them?

His hand was on the waistband of her slacks, fumbling with the fastening. "That's it, darling," he urged roughly as his own passion quickened. "You're mine now, all mine, and we're going to seal the matter once and for all."

Somehow his words pierced through the fog of desire that enfolded her. His, all his. It sounded as though he thought he was making a purchase. Just what did he think their lovemaking was going to prove? What did he think it was going to buy him?

She heard the zipper of her slacks descend and she reached to stop it. "Wait," she choked out, forcing herself to try to reach the surface of sanity from the pool of sensation she was drowning in.

"No, darling, we can't wait any longer." His words were slurred, as though he too was far from his normal control. "Now is the time." His hand plunged beneath the cloth, cupping her as though he already claimed ownership.

"No!" It took every bit of strength she possessed to force him away from her. "Stop it, Luke. I want you to stop."

Her determination finally came through to him and he hesitated. Drawing back, he looked at her a bit dazedly, then genuine concern swept across his face. "What is it? Did I hurt you?"

She wriggled out from beneath him and reached for her sweater, slipping it over her head before he could stop her. "Not really," she replied evenly as she closed her zipper and straightened her clothes. "Not in any way that the bruises will show."

He was frowning uncertainly. "What are you talking about?" he demanded, taking her wrist in an iron grip.

She raised her chin and glared into his eyes. "You deal in tempting currency, Luke Chisholm," she accused sharply, "but it's no sale this time."

She snapped her wrist away from his hold on her and rose to pace across the room. He stood up as well, coming after her with a quick stride.

"You're going to have to be a little more explicit, Jean," he said softly, his voice sheathed in a cloak of calm. "I'm afraid I don't quite understand your innuendos."

She backed against the swinging door that led to the kitchen. For the first time she was on the verge of being physically frightened of him. He was so big, so strong; she knew he could easily overpower her. If she made him really angry, she wouldn't have a chance.

Even so, she didn't moderate her own fury. She hated what he'd done to her and she was going to let him know it.

"Okay. I'll spell it out for you." She narrowed her gray eyes and pushed back the honey-colored hair that was drifting in wisps across her face. "You want Danni to win at the World Games. In order to do that, you need me out of the way. First you try to buy me with money and a job, then you try this." She gestured toward the couch. "Well, I'm sorry, Luke. I'm not for sale and neither is the championship."

His wide mouth twisted with scorn. "Don't be ridiculous. Nobody's trying to buy anything here."

"Oh, no?" She took hold of the medallion on her gold chain as though it would help her. "Then what do you call it?"

He stood loosely before her, his hands on his slim hips. "I called it a business proposition yesterday and I still call it that today."

"Is this the way you usually conduct business?" she asked sardonically. "You must have some reputation in your field." She shot him a sharp glance. "But then I guess it was all those years in football that did it. Can't get out of the habit of seducing every woman you meet, can you?"

His auburn brows were pulled together as though he was trying to puzzle out what her angle was. "I don't try to seduce every woman I meet, Jean," he said quietly. "In fact, you're the first woman who's seemed worth the effort in a long long time."

She wasn't going to listen to his compliments. That was exactly how she'd fallen into this in the first place.

"Making love to you has nothing to do with the business proposition," he went on. "My attraction to you is purely extracurricular. It just happened."

"Ah." She raised her eyebrows. "So conveniently timed, too. You came to the university intending to offer me a job yesterday, but once you heard me tell the press I had no intention of retiring, you put away that ploy and tried another."

Anger welled up in her again as she remembered how successful he'd been. "You used your charm and your scars to lure me into trusting you. You were going to take me up to your hotel room and pretend...all kinds of things."

She had trouble getting by that passage in her speech,

but she rushed ahead to keep him from interrupting the flow of her anger. "Then I suppose you would've sprung the real reason for having me there in the morning. Too bad Danni bumped into us and spoiled your plans."

He stood staring down at her, his face unreadable. For a moment she wondered if he'd heard a word she'd said, but then she saw the muscle twitch in his jawline and she noticed how tautly he was holding himself. His face was expressionless but there was an ill-concealed air of anger about him.

She shifted her weight nervously, fingered her medallion and wondered why he didn't answer her accusations. And then he was moving toward her so swiftly she didn't even have time to cry out before he'd swept her up in his arms.

He held her off the ground so that she reached for him recklessly to keep from falling, and while she was still off-balance his mouth took possession of hers in a kiss as fierce and wild as a desert wind.

The sweet sting of it sent a breath-stopping thrill surging through her body. She couldn't breathe; she couldn't think. She felt the force of his will and knew it could overwhelm her. It already very nearly had.

As suddenly as he had taken her, he let her go again. His mouth left hers and he dropped her back to the floor and stepped away, leaving her curiously cold and alone.

"Does that feel like make-believe, Jean?" he asked her harshly. "Do you really think I'm just pretending?"

She didn't know quite what to think at this point. She was still reeling from his kiss, leaning back against the kitchen door as though she was afraid the house was about to tip.

"Now let me tell you a few things," he went on firmly. "Wanting you as a coach for Danni and wanting you for myself are two very different goals. They have nothing to do with each other."

He stepped closer again. "But my first duty is to Danni. She has to have everything I can give her to win that championship. And I'm convinced you should think seriously about taking the job as her coach."

He put up a hand to stop the angry retort he could see forming in her eyes. "I'm an athlete too, Jean. I know how hard it is to give something up just because time is passing. I can sympathize with that will to win you have burning inside you." He took a deep breath. "You'll have to learn to channel those energies somewhere else. We all do."

"I know that," she snapped back, hardly mollified. "But I'm not going to quit until my time is up."

He winced. "Don't you think the clock has pretty well ticked out?" he asked quietly.

"No!" A huge lump had taken up temporary residence in the center of her throat, and she felt tears beginning to sting her eyes. "No!"

This was her biggest fear. No one understood about diving, about how it made her what she was. What would she do without it? Who would want her? Anger and panic combined to make her slightly irrational and she ran at Luke, her hands balled into fists as though to beat him away, beat back the things he'd said, beat them out of her mind.

His chest felt hard and impenetrable, but she hit him again and he didn't do a thing to stop her. She couldn't really see him any longer. His image swam before her as her eyes filled and overflowed. She hit him again and again, as though through him she could vanquish all her misery.

Something released inside her and to her utter shame a sob tore from her throat, and then his arms were around her, holding her gently against him, rocking her. He was talking soft nonsense, his face in her hair.

She cried as she hadn't since she was a child, a deep wrenching anguish that tore at her throat and hurt her chest. In her misery she clung to him, and he gave her more comfort than she ever could have imagined.

"It's all right, darling," he crooned, his hand cupping her cheek. "It hurts, but you're going to be all right."

The storm receded, but she didn't dare lift her head and look him in the eye. Her breathing became more regular, but still she hid against him, listening to his words.

He didn't understand. He never would. He wanted her to coach Danni. She was the one he really cared about. Danni, and possibly even her beautiful mother.

"You'd better go," she said at last, her voice muffled against his black sweater.

She felt him stiffen. "I want to stay, Jean," he said quietly. "I don't want to leave you alone like this."

She shook her head, pulling away and wiping her eyes without looking at him. "You'd better go," she repeated. "Please go. We have no more to say to each other."

For a moment she was afraid he was going to get angry again, and though she didn't look at him, she could feel him harnessing his explosive temper, though it took some effort.

"I think we have a lot more to say to each other," he stated plainly. "You need some time to think over the things we've discussed."

She heard him walking toward the front door, and finally she turned to look at him.

He wasn't smiling but he still had his ever-present confidence. "I'll be back, Jean," he promised, his hand on the doorknob. "I'm not going to let you forget me."

His blue-eyed gaze held hers for a long moment, then

he was gone and all she could hear was the sound of his heels beating a tattoo on the sidewalk.

Jean stood where she was, her eyes closed. How could she have lost control the way she had? She was terribly ashamed of what she'd done. She couldn't remember ever having opened her feelings so blatantly before, either sexually or in anger, as she'd done with Luke tonight. There was something about him that opened the floodgates of her emotions.

She didn't want to analyze what that might be. No, she had to get back to the business of forgetting him. But that wasn't easy to do when he kept popping up all over the place.

Suddenly she giggled. There'd been a song like that once, hadn't there? Something about, how can I miss you if you won't go away? Laughter bubbled in her throat and though it had a thread of hysteria running through it, she threw back her head and let it flow.

She was going to be all right. If she still had her sense of humor, she could do anything. Even learn to put Luke out of her mind.

"I'm not going to let you forget me," he'd said, almost as though he'd read her mind and recognized her intention. But there was nothing much he could do about it, she decided sternly. After all her years of diving, she was a master at concentration. If she determined to rid her mind of him, she would do it.

What could he do, mount some sort of seductive campaign to win her over? She smiled again. There was certainly very little chance of that. She was ready to p ry any of his moves.

THE FIRST RED ROSE arrived early the next morning. It was lying on top of her newspaper when she opened the door at the crack of dawn.

She stared down at it for a full sixty seconds before she reached out and picked it up. It had a very long stem. The flower itself was just a bud, barely showing signs of unfurling its blood-red petals. There was a card.

Dear Water Princess,
It's traditional to send a dozen red roses to one's lover. Are you my lover? You have three long days to practice making the right answer.

Jean put the beautiful bud to her lips. Her mind told her to throw it out with the morning's coffee grounds. Her heart coaxed her into letting it stay.

"Just for a little while," she promised herself as she pulled out a long-necked crystal vase and filled it with warm water. She snipped off an inch of the stem and stuck the flower in. "There's no reason to let a good rose go to waste."

She wondered only fleetingly why he talked about a dozen and then sent only one, but she quickly got the picture when a delivery boy arrived in the middle of afternoon practice and handed her another one.

"I'm not going to let you forget me," he'd said. So this was what he meant.

"Something from a secret admirer?" Eleanor asked with interest. A sudden light flashed across her face. "That Luke Chisholm! Is he the one who sent you this?"

Jean looked at her. "There's no card," she said evasively.

"Then it must be him." Eleanor nodded wisely. "You should've seen the way he was watching you dive yesterday." She laughed. "He was too much of a gentleman to let it show too blatantly, but there was pure lust oozing from every pore."

"Eleanor! Honestly!"

The small dark woman shrugged. "It's true. The man's after your bod, girl, and I think you ought to consider the offer." She rolled her dark eyes. "What a hunk!"

Jean was surprised to find hot color flooding her cheeks. "Are we going to practice some diving here or not?" she asked tartly, and Eleanor looked almost contrite.

The tables had been turned a bit ironically. Only that morning Eleanor had been reading Jean the riot act for her lack of dedication.

"We're not just playing around here, Jean," she'd told her on the telephone. "You've got to work twice as hard as you did last year if you want to retain your championship. Every girl in diving is gunning for you. You can't let your commitment falter, or you're through."

Jean agreed with every word Eleanor said, but she had little choice. The occasion for the outburst was her call to her coach telling her that she wouldn't be in until noon.

"I'm taking Bette around to meet with some physical therapists this morning," Jean had told her. "I'm sorry I forgot to warn you yesterday."

"That's an entire half day lost, Jean. Every half day you lose will show during competition."

Jean knew that, but Bette was her friend and she needed help. "We'll just have to accept that this time," she told Eleanor. "There's nothing I can do."

Eleanor seemed awfully touchy lately. She'd always been a tough taskmaster, but in recent months she seemed to have lost control of her temper, as well. Jean was afraid the two of them were going to have to sit down for a long talk sometime soon and straighten out whatever it was that bothered her coach.

But for now, Eleanor was enchanted with the single rose bud.

"Just a little piece of his heart," she mused, bending close to sniff the lovely fragrance. "But a little piece is better than nothing."

"What do you mean?" Jean asked warily.

"If a man gives you a dozen red roses, that means he gives you his heart," she said dreamily. "You'll really know where you stand if he shows up with the other eleven."

Jean put the rose down carefully near her towel. "Shall we get on with it?" she asked crisply, not about to tell Eleanor that she was afraid the rest of the dozen were surely on their way.

She might as well have gone home. The rose threw her concentration off just enough to ruin the workout. She couldn't keep from glancing into the bleachers every so often, just to see if she had any spectators, and that didn't help keep her attention on what she was doing.

But Eleanor didn't seem to notice. Her mind was on something far away, as well.

This was going to have to stop. The card that morning had said she had three days to make up her mind, and she'd read that almost with relief, thinking she had three days respite from the torment of her feelings for him.

But she'd been naïve to think that. She knew he was right when he said he was going to make sure she didn't forget him.

She was almost blasé when she found the third rose on her doorstep as she arrived home that evening. She'd been expecting it. She nonchalantly picked it up and carried it in to reside with the other two in the crystal vase.

Fixing herself a can of tomato-rice soup, she sat down to watch the evening television news. The national news followed events on the international scene and then the announcer went into local sports. When Danni's pretty face appeared on the screen, it took Jean a moment to adjust and begin listening to what the announcer was saying. As she listened, she put down her spoon and sat with hands clenched together.

". . . Danni Worth, the brightest star among all those young divers poised to challenge that grand old lady of diving, Jean Archer, for the right to wear the springboard crown. Tell us, Danni—" the microphone was shoved in front of Danni's pouty red mouth "—what brings you to Las Vegas?"

Jean groaned, wincing at the way she was being referred to these days, but she was interested to see just what Danni would tell the reporter.

Danni's smile was charming. She had a perfect combination of little-girl sweetness and tough know-how. All in all, the result came across as a model for a young Miss America.

"Of course, we're in Las Vegas mainly because we love it here. It's one of our favorite places to visit." She showed her straight white teeth to the camera, then the picture panned back, showing Sheila standing just behind her.

"As you know, the World Games are to be held here in July," Sheila said, leaning forward toward the mike. "We wanted Danni to become acclimatized to the area. We want to do everything we can to give her a chance at that championship."

"We wish you every bit of luck," the announcer was gushing. "You two look almost like sisters, did you know that?"

But Jean wasn't listening any longer. She'd noticed the masculine hand on Sheila's silk-covered arm, and her heart beat a loud dance in her chest while she held her breath, wondering if the camera would pan back further.

"All of Las Vegas will be rooting for you," the announcer assured them, ignoring the fact that Jean was the hometown contender. Then the picture broadened to show the pool area at the Camelot Hotel, and there was Luke, holding Sheila's arm and smiling down into her lovely upturned face.

The picture faded and was quickly replaced by a shot of a baby waddling in saggy diapers, frowning unhappily until a new style with elastic on the legs miraculously thrust him back on the ten-best-dressed-babies list, and brought a beatific smile to his baby lips.

But Jean didn't see that at all. Even though it was no longer on the screen, she still saw the handsome head of reddish brown hair turned toward Sheila, the large square hand on the slender arm.

Something was twisting like a knife in her heart and suddenly she knew what it was. She was jealous! She'd never felt quite like this before in her life. She was jealous. Did that mean she was also in love?

No!

She rose, switched off the set and took her bowl of barely touched soup back to the kitchen.

No, she refused to be in love. She had no time for it in the first place. And, in the second place, the consequences of falling into such a trap were much too terrifying.

Almost desperately she reached for the telephone and dialed Bette's number. Maybe Bette would like to take in a movie tonight, or just sit and talk. Anything to keep from thinking about Luke.

"Hello?"

The voice was unfamiliar to Jean and at first she thought she'd dialed the wrong number.

"This is the babysitter," the voice answered when she asked for Bette. "Ms Random won't be home until very late."

Jean frowned, puzzled. Bette rarely left Andy alone
for the evening and usually when she did, she left him
at Jean's, rather than hire a sitter to sit with him. At
his age, he was beginning to rebel against things like
that.

"May I talk to Andy please?" she asked the girl.

"Hi kid," she said when his adolescent voice came on
the line. "How are you doing?"

"Fine." She could hear the metal crutches clang
against the telephone table.

"I went with your mother today to pick out a therapist to help you get your legs back under you. Ed
Garvey, the man she chose, is going to be great, believe
me. He's been my instructor in a couple of classes and he
knows all there is to know about hydrotherapy."

Andy grunted with assumed disinterest.

Jean frowned, wondering if he was disturbed about
the new treatment. "Remember when I gave you swimming lessons when you were a kid?" she reminded him.
"It'll be a lot like that. You'll have fun."

"Maybe." There was a pause, and when he spoke
again his voice sounded years younger. "I wish you
were the one doing it."

She smiled into the receiver. At twelve he wavered so
between helpless child and cocky teenager. "I'm not
licensed yet, honey. Besides, you're going to like Mr.
Garvey a whole lot once you get to know him."

"I guess."

"Do you know what time your mother's going to get
home tonight?"

The pause on the other end of the line was dramatic.
"I'm not supposed to tell," he said at last.

"Well, all right." She laughed, not sure if this was
some aberration of Andy's or Bette's real order to her
son. "Far be it from me to make you divulge the secret.

Just tell her I called and that I'll be up until midnight if she wants to call me when she gets home."

So much for a movie. Eleanor and Mike wouldn't appreciate her breaking in on their night with the books of Mike's business. That left homework or a good book. The television would stay off. She wouldn't risk seeing Danni's smiling face again, promising shining victories at Jean's expense. Or seeing Luke's hand on Sheila's arm. . . .

The peal of her front doorbell stabbed through her like a bolt of electricity. She had to reach out against the wall to steady herself before she could turn and start to walk toward the door. With her hand on the knob, she took a deep relaxing breath, closed her eyes and flung open the door.

7

"Hı ya, Toots." Jeffrey stood on her doorstep, his grin as wide as ever. "Saw your light and thought I'd pop in for a little chat." He raised an eyebrow. "Is the coast clear?"

She sagged against the doorway, relief sweeping through her like an ocean breeze. "Come on in. I've been wanting to talk to you, too."

He walked in, peering around with comical exaggeration. "Where is he?" he asked in a loud stage whisper. "And does he or does he not have his pants on?"

"Who?" she asked curtly, though she knew very well whom he was talking about.

Jeffrey swung around, a twisted grin on his face. "Who?" he mocked her. "Who do you think? The man who told me he was going to sweep you off your feet and carry you away into the sunset."

He frowned. "Or is it sunrise? I never could keep that straight." Shrugging, he flopped down on her couch. "I guess that's why I've always had such trouble carrying women off. I can never remember what time of day I'm supposed to do it."

Jean felt a pang of conscience. She'd thought for a long time that she and Jeffrey were well matched, but she'd found out there was more to the male-female relationship than that, and she knew they'd never been anything but good friends. He'd claimed to be ready to break off anything more serious when Luke had asked him at dinner the other night, but Jean wondered if the bluntness of it all had hurt him. She hoped not, but she wasn't sure what she could do to soften the break.

"If you're talking about Luke Chisholm," she said evenly, sitting down beside him, "he's not here." She glared at her friend. "And he wouldn't be wandering around with his pants off if he were."

Jeffrey snorted. "You wanna bet? I saw the way the man was looking at you. Little Red Riding Hood had a better chance."

Jean lifted her head and stared into middle space musingly. "Little Red Riding Hood helped chop off the wolf's head in the end," she said speculatively, then raised an eyebrow to Jeffrey. "All she needed was a friendly passing woodsman."

Jeffrey's mouth fell open and he pointed to his own chest in disbelief. "This ain't no woodsman, lady. If you want Luke Chisholm's head to roll, you better get yourself another man."

They grinned at each other, suddenly back on the old familiar footing. Jeffrey reached out to take her hand in his.

"Now tell me, Red," he said, "what's that Big Bad Wolf done to you?"

She looked searchingly at his open face, wondering just how much she should tell him. "He didn't carry me off into the sunset, for starters," she said slowly, feeling her way. "It turned out he was referring to a change of career, not a world-shaking romance."

Jeffrey frowned. "Come again?"

She looked down at their intertwined hands. "The big surprise was he's Danni Worth's guardian. They want me to quit and coach her for the World Games."

"Oh. And of course you went into catatonic shock at the thought of it."

She pulled her hand away from his. "Do you blame me?" she flared.

He shook his head. "Let's just say I understand," he said slowly. Then he grimaced. "Jean, why don't you at least consider it? After all, coaching the next champ would be a great way to cap off a career."

"No." She flung herself up off the couch and began pacing the room. "No. Why can't any of you people get it through your heads? I'm not a coach. Coaching isn't anything like diving."

His eyes were troubled. "Jean, you're not superwoman. You can't dive forever."

She clenched her hands into fists. She'd never claimed to be superwoman, but she was one of the best divers in the world. Why couldn't anyone understand what that meant to her? Why did they all push so hard for her to quit? She knew she was still as good as she'd ever been—no—better! And yet everyone thought she should give it up.

None of the men in her life had ever wanted to come in second to diving. None of them had been willing to tolerate the demands of constant training. There was no use in even dreaming of being able to sustain a relationship. It just didn't work.

"Maybe I can't dive forever, but I can keep it up as long as my body responds. I'm not anywhere near ready to quit yet." Quitting would be like dying. And how many people did that voluntarily?

"Okay." He spread his hands wide. "Okay, you win. Dive your little heart out. But sit back down here and relax, would you? I can't talk to a kangaroo in motion."

She slumped back down beside him. "Oh, Jeffrey, why can't everyone just leave me alone and let me dive?"

"You've got it bad for Luke, don't you?"

She stared into his eyes, then slowly shook her head. She could keep control. She had to. Luke Chisholm wanted only two things from her and he wasn't going to get either one. "There's nothing between us," she said evenly.

Jeffrey looked skeptical. "Nothing? You can't tell me the guy was only interested in business, because I won't buy it. I saw the way—"

"Nothing!" she interrupted. "I can't let him ruin my concentration. You know that."

Jeffrey knew that only too well. He made a face that revealed a tracing of the pain he must have felt in the past. "Yeah? Lots of luck, Little Red Riding Hood."

Jean stared miserably at her creeping charlie, thinking abstractedly that it needed a trim, and suddenly she realized Jeffrey wasn't saying anything. She couldn't remember a time when he'd let such a long silence grow between them. Curious, she looked up to see what he was doing.

Jeffrey was glancing around the room restlessly, looking from one thing to another uncomfortably. Jean didn't think she'd ever seen him do that before. It was a night for firsts.

"What's the matter?" she asked him, concerned.

He stared at her as though this was going to take a major effort. "I've been trying to think of a way to tell you this for weeks now and there never seems to be a way. I thought if you and Luke had something going, it would be easier, but now . . . well, I've got to get it out in the open, and the only way I know how is to use my normal crass tactless bad manners." He took a deep breath while she frowned at him in puzzlement. "Want to go to an engagement party?" he asked in a rush.

She shrugged. "Whose?"

He winced. "Mine."

Her jaw dropped. "Yours?" she repeated.

He nodded in mock misery. "I haven't asked her yet, but I'm going to." He cowered against the corner of the couch as though she was about to hit him. "Forgive me, forgive me!" he cried. "I couldn't help myself."

Jean was caught between her original shock and a sense of amusement at his obvious embarrassment. "Do you mean to tell me you've been going out with another girl and you didn't even tell me?"

It wasn't unusual for either one of them to have a casual date or two with someone else, but neither ever kept it a secret.

He nodded contritely. "I didn't even tell you. I was scared to even tell myself. I didn't dare think about her too much for fear she'd evaporate on me." He turned toward her, enthusiasm firing his eyes. "Jean, she's perfect. She has no career. She laughs at my jokes. She loves me. She's a doctor's daughter, so she knows what it means to be a doctor's wife."

Jean shook her head, wondering how this could be perfection. "What's her name?"

"Mindy."

"Sounds like an after-dinner mint."

"I know. Ain't it great?"

"Ain't it?" Jeffrey was in love with another woman. Somehow that possibility had never entered her mind. But now that it had, she realized what a good thing it was. Suddenly she started to laugh. "Oh, Jeffrey. As long as you love her. As long as she treats you with the kindness you deserve."

They hugged and she was glad for him, even though the gladness was tainted by the tiniest shred of sadness at losing the whole of his friendship.

"We'll still be friends, won't we?" she asked him.

"Sure." He grinned. "After all, that's all we've ever

been." He sighed, looking her up and down. "It's too bad we never got physical, Jean," he said sadly. "I'm beginning to find I'm a master at the game." He threw back his shoulders and narrowed his eyes with manufactured arrogance. "If you'd only given me a chance, I could've played your body like a fine ka-zoo."

She laughed. "You think we could've made sweet jug-band music, do you? Knowing us, the sound would've been definitely discordant." She pushed him toward the door. "Out. I've got a six o'clock workout."

She knew she was going to miss the closeness of their past. She'd depended on Jeffrey for so long. But she was glad he was going to be happy. She knew she could never give him the sort of devotion he needed.

Sighing, she turned out the lights one by one and pre-pared to go to bed. It had been a long day. A day when she hadn't seen Luke except on a television screen. Why was it that she felt as though the day had been filled with him?

She stepped into her bedroom, pulled off her sweater and slacks, draped them over the back of a chair and turned toward her bed. For one moment she stood there in shock. Then she grabbed her robe, held it to her chest and whirled, looking in every shadow. There was no one there. But someone had been.

Her neatly made bed had been turned down and a ruby-red rosebud lay on her white pillow. Luke had left his stamp again.

SHE DROPPED a cup of coffee right on the middle of her counter the next morning. It slipped out of her hand for no reason at all—except maybe that Luke was driving her crazy. The cup shattered and brown stains splashed all over her yellow sweater. Mumbling a few choice words, she mopped up the mess and went back into her bedroom to change into a different top.

"Luke Chisholm," she swore softly, "you're going to pay for this."

When she finally opened her front door, the rose was on top of the newspaper, just as she'd expected.

"Actually, I'm surprised I didn't wake up to find it between my teeth," she muttered to herself as she poured a fresh cup of coffee and spread the paper out flat to read the morning news.

Five rose buds sat in her crystal vase. What had Eleanor said the day before? An even dozen and you've got him by the heart. Jean smiled wryly. Fat chance of that.

She turned to the sports section and quickly wished she hadn't. Danni's cute smile took up a good quarter of the front page. "New Diving Queen?" the headline asked.

Involuntarily her fingers clawed across the page, crumpling the paper. It took a half hour of yoga positions to restore her normal good humor, and by then she was late for her morning workout.

But Eleanor hardly seemed to notice. She was on the telephone when Jean showed up and didn't complete her conversation until Jean was well into her warm-up exercises.

"On the phone with Mike again?" she asked as Eleanor helped strap her into the harness for the trampoline. "You two just can't get enough of each other, can you?"

"Guess not." Eleanor seemed cold and unapproachable. "Here, lean back a little so I can pull this belt tighter."

Jean couldn't stand it any longer. She was sure something was wrong. "Eleanor," Jean began hesitantly, "if there's anything you'd like to talk about . . . . I mean, if you and Mike are having problems . . . ."

Eleanor gave the belt a savage pull and looked up at Jean, her eyes blazing. "If you really must know, you're the problem."

Jean frowned. "What?" At first she thought Eleanor must be joking.

Eleanor sighed. "Oh, Jean, you are the problem. I can't go on doing this forever. It takes all my time, all my energy. I wasn't going to tell you until after the World Games, but since it's come up—I'm quitting as soon as the games are over."

"Quitting?" The word stuck like a sharp spike in her throat. "You can't quit. We're a team. How am I going to train without you?"

Eleanor shook her head wearily. "I never expected it to go on this long and you know it. After all, I gave up my diving career at twenty-two to take on coaching you full time. You're twenty-eight and still going strong."

Reading the stricken look on Jean's face, Eleanor seemed to feel a flood of remorse. She reached out and put a hand on Jean's arm.

"I want to have a real marriage, Jean. Can't you understand that? I want to spend my days helping my husband build his business instead of going over diving turns. I want to spend my evenings reading baby books instead of manuals on physical development. How can I go about making a family when I've got to be away every other weekend for a meet in some far-off city?"

When Jean didn't answer, she went on. "I'm thirty-four years old. It's time for me to go on to something else, don't you think? If I'm going to do it at all, it better be soon."

Jean felt as though she'd been hit in the stomach. She'd never expected this. No one else understood, but

Eleanor always had. If Eleanor left her, there would be no one.

"I'm sorry you feel that way," Jean told her stiffly. "You should have made your wishes clear before this." Hurt, she wanted to add, *Why don't you just go ahead and quit now—I'll get someone else to coach me.* But she didn't dare. There was no one else. Without Eleanor, she'd never win in July.

She and Eleanor had always been so close it was hard to believe she could have been harboring these feelings without Jean ever guessing. She wanted to reach out to her, to tell her she was sorry to have been the cause of trouble between her and her husband, but at the same time she felt a knife thrust of betrayal and the pain would have to lessen before she would be able to do that.

Eleanor searched her eyes, then sighed and drew her hand away. "Well, at least it's out in the open now. Let's get to work."

Jean needed concentration desperately and it was getting more and more difficult to find. Everything in her life was turning upside down. The only thing she could think of that might save her was a total retreat into the depths of her competitive spirit. It took all her energy, but she managed to do a pretty good job of it.

She withdrew, hardly seeing or hearing Eleanor any longer. All she heard was her own voice, her own rhythms. She practiced very hard on the trampoline, and after a quick jog to her class and then a period of meditation in the back room, she was ready to practice her dives.

The rose arrived right on time, about an hour into the workout. Jean took it from the delivery boy and flung it down with her things alongside the pool. Something made her turn and look at the bleachers on the other side. Luke was sitting there, watching her.

She stared at him for a tense moment, then ignoring Eleanor's question as to where she was going, she began the long march around the pool to where he sat.

As she strode across the cement deck, water spraying from every step, he began to personify all the anger and frustration she'd endured for the last few days. Everything was going wrong, and it had all begun when he'd stepped in to turn her head and throw her goals awry.

As she neared him she could see that he was dressed in brushed denim, looking very Western with his jacket open to reveal the hard muscles of his chest under the crisp white shirt. His tan had darkened since she'd seen him last and his blue eyes looked startlingly brilliant in his dark face.

She stopped in front of where he sat, three seats up from the front of the stands, suddenly realizing she had no towel or anything else to protect her scantily clad body from his scrutiny. But she brushed that thought aside and placed her hands angrily on her hips.

"You are ruining my life!" she bit out at him. "You're going to have to stop it."

He stared back at her for a moment without saying anything, his face unreadable. Finally, he tilted his head and narrowed his eyes. "I warned you I was going to change things. You haven't really seen anything yet."

"Luke, you can't do this. I'm a diver. That's what I am, that's my identity. But I can't dive when I can't concentrate." She passed a nervous hand through her wet dripping hair. "And I've never met a bigger distraction than you!"

His face relaxed into something very close to a smile and he slowly began to unwind his long body from the bench. "You may be a diver, Jean," he said firmly, "but that's not your identity."

He stepped down over the rows and suddenly he was

before her, his hand touching her shoulder. "You're a woman," he told her with rounded emphasis that turned the word into something golden and desirable. Now both his hands were on her shoulders and he was drawing her near. "You're a woman first and foremost. And I'm going to prove that to you right now."

She was dripping wet and his suit was obviously expensive, but he pulled her up against him as though that didn't matter at all. Her skin was chilled from the water; he was as warm as the desert sun.

She tried to protest as his mouth came down on her cool lips, but her words only gave him the entrance he needed to get to the heart of her sweetness. His tongue slid along hers in an explosion of fire and his cheek warmed the skin of hers.

Forgetting all about the fact that Eleanor was standing on the other side of the pool watching and that half the swim team was by now forming an interested audience on the far side of the stadium, she kissed him back, clinging to him with reckless abandon.

When he finally drew back, she stared up at him, groggy with the feelings he'd unleashed.

He took her chin in his hand and raised it. "You make the judgment, Jean," he said in his husky drawl. "What is it that you want right now? What a diver wants, or what a woman wants?"

She couldn't seem to tear her gaze from his and she wasn't sure she really wanted to. "You are ruining my life," she whispered to him again, and he grinned.

"Good," he said emphatically. "Your life needs ruining."

She swallowed hard. "You said you'd give me three days," she complained shakily, grasping at straws. "It's only been two."

He cocked a dark eyebrow. "You're right. I'm not here to see you."

"You're not?"

He shook his head. "No. George Parness, the aquatic director here at the university, gave us permission to let Danni practice here while she's in Las Vegas. I came over to help get that set up."

"Danni? Here?" The thought was totally unsettling.

He smiled. "You won't mind, will you?"

"Who, me?" She pulled away from his hand, starting to feel like her old self again. "Why should I mind? This town has all but named Danni queen of the may. Who am I to object?"

"Jean. . . ." He started to reach for her again, his eyes darkened with concern, and she spun away. But before she had a chance to escape, Sheila was closing in on her position and she could see Danni advancing toward the board.

"Jean Archer, just the person I've wanted to see." Sheila came forward, hand outstretched, a completely guileless smile on her beautiful face. Jean took her hand and glanced at Luke, wondering if Sheila had witnessed the kiss they'd just exchanged, wondering just what the relationship was between the two of them, anyway.

"I hope you've had time to think over our offer," Sheila was saying. "Now don't say a word if you haven't been convinced yet, because I know Luke has more ammunition up his sleeve to bring you around." She laughed warmly and Jean managed a tight smile.

"I'm in the middle of a workout," she said, edging away. "Please excuse me, I do have to get back." She waved to Danni. "Nice to see you again." She was amazed at how natural she sounded. "Goodbye."

Out of the corner of her eye she could see Luke coming toward her, but she evaded him and hurried off.

Eleanor must have surmised that there was something very wrong for she didn't ask any questions or make any comments as Jean took the board again. Once more she was able to dig deep inside and block out the world. She never even looked down at the other end of the pool where Danni was practicing, nor did she glance once at the bleachers. By the time she was finished, all the others had left.

"See you tomorrow, won't I?" she said to Eleanor as she began to gather her things.

"Of course," Eleanor said.

Jean looked down at the rose lying beside her bag. She wanted to grind it into the floor with her heel. Ammunition indeed! But something stopped her from destroying the beautiful flower. Instead, she carried it home, just as she had the other the day before.

The seventh rose lay on her doorstep and she ran right into her bedroom to check for the eighth, but the bed was untouched. She sighed with relief.

The evening seemed to drag on forever. She didn't dare turn on the television. Danni might have been elected mayor of the city by now, and if so, she didn't want to hear about it.

Jeffrey would probably be with his beloved Mindy tonight. Funny how that didn't really bother her at all. And Eleanor wouldn't want to hear from her. Jean's clear impression was that Mike would be even less pleased with a spontaneous visit from the woman who took up most of his wife's time. She tried calling Bette, but her good friend was out again.

"How was your first session with Ed Garvey?" she asked Andy when he came to the phone.

"Okay," was his noncommittal answer. "He doesn't like horses."

Jean frowned, knowing Andy would think him a heretic for that. "How do you know?"

Andy sighed with deep resignation. "He said if all the horses in the world suddenly were extinct, it would be okay with him. He thinks they break too many kids' bones, and that I shouldn't ride again."

Jean bit her lip. The whole point was to get him well enough to ride again, at least in his mind. It didn't sound like Garvey was a master at psychological motivation. Perhaps she and Bette would have to look further.

"You just keep up the good work, honey," she told him. "And tell your mother to call me when she gets back from her mysterious whatever."

"Okay," he said more cheerfully. "But she won't. She'll just say it's too late."

Jean knew that was probably true, but Bette's whereabouts was beginning to intrigue her. In the meantime, she was alone again.

She fixed herself a tuna sandwich and tried hard not to think about Luke or Danni or the problem with Eleanor. She did some overdue homework, read a diving magazine that had come in the mail and spent some time watering her plants, wandering around the apartment and out on her little patio with a long-necked watering can, murmuring encouraging words to her greenery.

Finally it was late enough to go to bed and she puttered around in her bathroom, singing a popular tune at the top of her lungs while she prepared for bed.

Singing usually made her feel better. She couldn't always hit the high notes and sometimes the tune got lost while she fumbled for a word, but it still cheered her and she stepped into her bedroom feeling almost happy again.

The song died in her throat as she stared at her bed.

The covers were turned back and a red rose lay on her pillow.

She swallowed hard, backing against her bathroom door. "Luke?" she whispered, peering around the edges of her room. "Luke?" she said louder.

There was no answer. She held her breath. There was no sound.

Slowly she ventured out into the room, then into the hall. The rooms were strange in the darkness. She imagined him standing against a wall, moved one step closer and then saw it was just a trick of the moonlight.

"Luke?" she called again.

She rounded the corner into her living room and immediately saw the drapes billowing. The sliding glass door was open. She knew she hadn't left it open, but she must have left it unlocked after she had been out on the patio, watering her flowers.

She ran out, padded across the cold stones with her bare feet, then leaned out over the railing and searched the night. There was no sign of life.

"Luke Chisholm, I hate you," she called into the shadows. But when she retreated back into her apartment and locked her sliding glass door there was a smile curving her lips.

8

THE NEXT DAY was full of surprises, beginning with the absence of a rose on her morning paper. She stared at where it wasn't, drew back and closed the door, forgetting to pick up her paper, then had to open it again and step out. She looked furtively up and down the street, then into the bushes on either side of her entryway. No rose.

"Number nine, where are you?" she muttered, then grabbed her paper and went inside, hoping there was no one watching her strange antics.

She was so sure a rose would arrive during her practice that she was stunned to see the time on the stadium clock after she'd finished her required dives. Two o'clock in the afternoon, and no roses.

You needed a dozen to have a chance at his heart, didn't you, she thought to herself bemusedly as she made her way to the locker room a bit later. Maybe he'd decided to stop before he gave it away.

Another surprise came in the form of Danni Worth. The girl was waiting to talk to her by her locker.

"Hi, Jean," she said, grinning impishly. "I've been wanting to talk to you alone." She stepped closer, squinting with the effort at saying just what she meant. "I'm sorry about practicing here at the same pool where you're based. The others don't understand, but I know how you must feel to have me horning in."

Jean was disarmed against her will. The girl was quite

serious. How much more satisfying it would have been to be able to hate her!

"It doesn't bother me," she reassured her. "My concentration can block out almost anything."

"Good." She grinned again. "I promised Luke I wouldn't hound you about being my coach, but I just want to tell you I really hope you agree to do it. You're the best and that's what I want to be, too."

Jean couldn't hold back an answering smile. She took her clothes out of her locker, then turned back. "Luke thinks a lot of you," she told the girl. "You're lucky to have someone who believes in you that way." A sudden memory of Uncle Max floated through her thoughts.

"I know. He's the greatest. Ever since daddy died he's been there for me, no matter what." She sighed, her pretty mouth pouting. "If only he'd marry my mother, everything would be perfect."

Jean's hands suddenly felt clammy. She turned back to her locker, unable to face Danni. "Is that . . . is that a real possibility?" She hated herself for stooping to this level, but she had to know.

Danni threw out her hands in childish abandon. "Who knows? I've certainly been working on it for ages." She grinned again and began to whirl away. "We'll only be here for a few more days and then you'll have your pool back." She stopped at the corner of a bank of gray lockers and looked at her. "Only I hope you'll be going to San Francisco with us when we leave." With a wave, she disappeared.

Jean dressed in a soft yellow shirt and navy blue slacks and left, driving home quickly, trying not to anticipate a rose on her doorstep.

Of course, there won't be one, she told herself sternly. *He's given up. He's decided to call it a lost cause, now that I've finally convinced him I won't give up diving.*

Besides, with Sheila waiting in the wings, why should he bother with a stubborn diver who refuses to do what he wants? If I was smart, I'd erase him from my mind and never think of him again.

The thought cut like a knife, but she knew it would be best that way. No, she mustn't expect a rose. If she did, she would only be hurt.

Yet a small piece of her heart was hoping to see a splash of deep red in front of her door, and more than a small piece was disappointed when the stoop was bare of any flower.

She couldn't eat a bite of dinner and she didn't feel up to calling anyone this night. She spent most of the time roaming her house, checking to see that all the doors were locked. As darkness fell she had to admit that it was time to let her hopes die a natural death.

Hopes, she asked herself, what hopes? If you were hoping for something like Luke Chisholm, you're a fool. A man like that who could have any beautiful woman in the world. . . .

The loud ring of her doorbell interrupted her internal harangue and she froze, hand to her throat. After a pause, the bell rang again. Slowly, like a sleepwalker, she went toward the sound. She pulled open the door and stared into Luke's enigmatic blue eyes.

He was wearing a plaid shirt, open at the neck, and faded jeans. He could have been any cowboy off the streets of a Western town, yet with the last light of the setting sun shimmering around him like a halo, she thought he'd never looked more seductive.

"Your three days are up," he said without preamble. He held the last four roses out to her.

Jean backed away from the bouquet, irrationally avoiding what they meant to them both symbolically.

Luke took advantage of her retreat to step inside and kick the door shut behind him.

"It's time to face facts. Jean," he said with barely restrained impatience, throwing the flowers down on her table and advancing toward her. "You've hesitated long enough."

"Luke, wait." She backed against the wall and slid along it, keeping just out of his reach. Her heart was beating so loudly she could hardly breathe. "What are you doing?"

He caught her with a hand in her thick hair, pulling her back against him. "Establishing territorial rights," he answered with silky arrogance.

She struggled against him. "I won't coach Danni," she cried, twisting to try to free herself. "I won't!"

"Do you think I care about that right now?" He forced her to face him. "All I care about is you and me."

A shudder ran through her body and he frowned, feeling it. "You and me," he repeated. "Get used to it."

His mouth took hers in a demanding kiss while his fingers unwound from her hair and went to the buttons on her shirt, pulling them apart, one by one, while she tried futilely to stop him.

"Luke, no," she moaned against his lips. "Stop a minute, let me think."

"No." He snapped the last button hard so that it popped from the material. "You think much too much. That's your problem."

He slid her shirt back, exposing her shoulders. Bending forward he drew a sensuous line across her collarbone with his tongue.

"Luke. . . ."

"If I let you think," he continued, "you'll think about reasons why we shouldn't do this." His tongue curled around her shoulder, then he removed the shirt completely and his fingers went to the front clasp on her lacy bra.

"And we're going to do this," he said softly. "That's no longer a question, Jean. It's a statement of fact."

Her bra fell away and she tried to cover her breasts, but he skillfully avoided her arms and leaned down to touch first one, then the other rosy-brown nipple with his tongue.

"Luke, we should talk first." Her words had little meaning to either of them, but she said them, almost as though the saying was a ritual she had to go through. She flattened herself against the wall, but he followed, pressing his hard body to hers in sensual persuasion.

"Talk all you want," he told her, his breath hot against her neck. "Just don't expect me to listen."

He had the calm strength of a man who knew exactly what he wanted and had no doubt he was going to get it. Suddenly she didn't doubt it either. A strange warmth was seeping slowly up from her legs, filling her with tingling delight, sapping what little will to resist she had left, and without warning she found herself stretching up, her arms around his neck, her body arched to take in every hard angle he possessed.

"My darling water princess," he whispered into her soft hair as it swirled around his face. "I feel like I've waited a lifetime for this."

She couldn't answer him. She heard small animal sounds and realized dimly that they were coming from her own throat. The room was spinning in a kaleidoscope of shadows and colors, and when she felt his knee thrust between her legs, gently parting them, it didn't seem to be an invasion, but a welcome progression that was right and natural.

She found herself kissing the tight lines of his neck, running her tongue along every ridge, nipping softly at

the tender skin in the hollow. Her fingers trembled as
she worked at the buttons of his shirt, pulling back the
material so that she could get at more of him. Her
mouth slid across his flesh, lips, teeth, tongue, glorying
in the feel of his masculine hardness. Something wild
was growing inside her and she wanted to devour him
with her love.

"That's it, princess," he growled as his own need
quickened. "You have all of me and I'll have all of you,
and that way we'll become one."

He loosened the belt of her pants and plunged both
hands down inside to curl around her bottom, then
lifted her up against him so that her naked breasts were
pressed to his shirtless chest and her hips were caught in
the cradle of his. She felt the flare of his passion and
gasped at the excitement that shot through her in cas-
cading waves that threatened to drown her with sensation.

She was cast adrift in a sea of sensuality that was new
to her, like nothing she'd ever experienced before. She
wasn't sure if she would ever make it back to shore. She
wasn't sure if she cared. She could be happy to go on
forever this way, drifting in the swells of his passion,
riding the crest of her own.

His hands were moving across her skin, conjuring up
quivering delight in places she wouldn't have dreamed
such things could exist. She moaned when he touched
her breasts and rubbed the dark tips to make them swell
with longing.

"Oh, Luke, please...."

She wasn't sure just what she was asking, but he
seemed to know.

"In a minute, princess," he murmured. "In just a
minute."

Suddenly she was up in his arms and he was carrying

her down the hall to her room. He kicked open the door and entered, laying her gently down on her burgundy bedspread and removing her slacks and panties before she realized his intention.

But she didn't mind. She felt no embarrassment in lying naked before his hungry gaze. Some basic feminine instinct made her aware of just how to move, how to set her body so as to strike a balance between modesty and enticement.

He stared down at her and reaching over, he cupped her navel with his palm before moving down slowly, exquisitely, to explore her more fully. She writhed at his touch, shuddering. He straightened and began pulling his belt from his jeans while she lay back, watching him. He pulled off his boots, then let his pants drop to the floor, and she held her breath, stunned by the beauty of his body as the evening light turned it into a stark landscape of luminosity and shadow.

But when he lowered himself to her and she felt the length of his naked flesh against the softness of her own, warmth melting against warmth, heat inciting response, she knew true ecstasy for the first time in her life.

"Now, Luke, now," she demanded, wrapping her legs around him as the driving pulse became overwhelming. At his entry, she sighed with satisfaction and met his rhythm. He kissed her, his breath coming faster, but he seemed to be holding back, as though afraid to rush her. She moaned and writhed beneath him, too aroused to wait, and he looked down at her in surprise, but her nails digging into his buttocks urged him on and he quickly joined her urgency, surging again and again as the pounding of their blood merged in a river of passion, turning them truly into one, two parts of a whole, both lover and beloved.

Together they rode the river, letting it hurl them

through the white-water rapids, gasping as it tossed them high, crying out as they came down again, and at the end, Jean heard a cry so loud it might have been a scream.

As she slowly regained her breath and let her body recapture its strength, she realized with warm embarrassment that the scream had been her own.

Luke shifted weight so that his long body lay next to hers, and she nestled her face into his shoulder, hoping she'd never have to come up and face him.

"Hi," he said softly, his hand stroking her hair. "How are you doing?"

Wonderful, she might have cried out. *Fabulous. Better than anything, ever. Even diving.* She caught her breath and closed her eyes. *Even diving.*

But she didn't say all that aloud. "Fine," she whispered instead, her voice muffled by his shoulder.

His hand crept in to find her cheek and cup it. "You didn't tell me you were such a wanton woman," he muttered. "I should have let you seduce me much earlier."

She pressed harder against him, not sure whether to be embarrassed or not. She'd never felt so passionate with a man before, but she didn't know how to tell him that. Was a woman supposed to tell a man exactly how she felt? Or was it safer to keep still and let him assume whatever he wanted?

They lay together for a long moment, both quite still. Suddenly Luke exploded. "Fine," he mimicked sarcastically. "Just fine! Blast!" He rolled over and glared down at her. "If 'fine' is all it was, why did we bother?"

She stared up at him wide-eyed, unable to think of a thing to say.

"Listen," he said hoarsely, "it was a lot more than 'fine' for me. It was possibly the most profound moment of my life, so far. So I won't let you get away with 'fine.'

I want to know it was better than that, or by God we'll
keep at it until it is."

He wanted to hear the words, and she had them ready
now. "It was definitely more than fine," she acceded,
and watched the fierceness fade from his eyes. "It
was...." She licked her dry lips, avoiding his gaze,
gathering strength. "It was like they always say it is in
the romances. You know, like you always hope, only it
never quite seems that way in real life. Only this
time...." She ended in a whisper. "This time it was."

He didn't say a word, but his fingers tightened on her
shoulder, tightened so hard she almost had to tell him he
was hurting her. Slowly she raised her head to meet his
gaze. His blue eyes were laughing and she wasn't shy
any longer. With sudden candor she tossed back her
hair and smiled into his face.

I love you, her smile said. Did she dare say it with
words?

He smiled back, then closed his eyes and stretched.
"So this is what your bed feels like. I've been anticipat-
ing this for three days."

She laughed, but she couldn't hold back a stray
twinge of skepticism. Luke Chisholm was the epitome of
what thousands of girls thought they wanted. No matter
how much he'd enjoyed the love they'd just made, she
couldn't believe it was really so special to him. He'd had
his pick. Could it be possible that a man like this might
have mooned over her like a lovesick Romeo? Somehow
she doubted it. But it was nice of him to pretend.

And if he could pretend, so could she. "Is that why
you came in to check it out last night?" she asked, raising up on her elbow to look down at his face.

"I wasn't 'checking it out,'" he answered, affronted.
"I was merely delivering your rose."

She grinned and threaded her fingers through the

thick curly hair on his chest. "I was a little worried, until
I figured out how you got in." She looked at him quiz-
zically. "How did you get in the first time?"

He smiled as though he was very pleased with himself. "Your apartment manager let me in."

"What?"

"Oh, don't blame her. I gave her a very romantic
story and she followed me into your room to be sure the
only thing I did was turn down your bed and lay the
rose on your pillow. Then she herded me right out."

She shook her head. "That first night wasn't so bad,
but the second night—you scared me to death."

He lifted a skeptical eyebrow. "Are you kidding?
Anyone who can belt out a song the way you do in your
bathroom couldn't be scared of anything."

"You heard me!" She curled her hand into a fist and
playfully pummeled his chest. "That was strictly
private. You had no right to listen."

His eyes danced with mischief. "Just grant me the
right not to have to hear you again and I'll beg your for-
giveness."

She sniffed, turning from him, but he caught her and
pulled her back down upon him. "Don't leave me,
Jean," he said huskily, suddenly serious. "I want to keep
your body touching mine for as long as I can."

She spread out over him, her hands running silkily
down the inner skin of his outstretched arms, her legs
lining his. She felt such a welling up of emotion that she
had to hide her face again to keep him from seeing the
tears brimming in her eyes. She'd never felt so loved
nor so loving.

"A mountain spring," he murmured suddenly.
"That's what you remind me of."

"What?" She lifted her head to look into his face.
"What are you talking about?"

His forefinger traced the contour of her face while he told her. "When I was still in college, I went hiking once in the desert mountains out by the Saline Valley in California. We'd been hiking all day, trying to find a stand of bristlecone pine—you know those ancient trees—that a friend of mine, a botanist, was sure was out there. We were tired and thirsty, just about out of water, and I was getting the idea that we were possibly lost."

He laughed softly, remembering. "I was beginning to notice the vultures circling. Things were getting grim." His hand opened and cupped her cheek. "We were pretty high up on a ridge and my foot slipped. I started sliding down to the rocks below, losing control, going faster all the time. I was pretty sure I was in big trouble."

He took a deep breath. "I came crashing through the brush and all of a sudden I was in a hidden canyon. The brush stopped my fall without too much damage. And there, rushing through the heart of this canyon, was the most beautiful mountain spring you ever saw." He smiled at her. "The water was cool and clear and clean and I lay right down in it. It slipped around me like a silver caress." His hand thrust back to stab into her hair. "And that's the way you are."

He pulled her down to meet his kiss that started out a gesture of simple affection and soon became something much more.

"Oh, Luke," she gasped, slipping down off him and rolling a bit away. She didn't know why, but to her mind there seemed something slightly illicit about such a quick encore and she resisted it, as much as she was tempted.

Luke raised up on his elbow. "That's okay," he said softly. "We've got all night."

All night. The thought sent a shock wave through

her. He was planning to stay all night. He was planning to sleep with his arms wrapped around her, her body curled against his. She gazed back at what she could see of him in the gathering gloom. "All night?" she asked, wanting to make sure.

He was fumbling with her reading lamp on the headboard, and then he switched it on, flooding their area with a golden light that lent them the colors found in old masters' paintings.

"All night," he repeated firmly. "And in the morning we'll go to my suite at the hotel."

"Oh, no," she said quickly. "I can't miss practice."

He reached for her, running his hand along the slope of her hip. "Yes, you can," he told her calmly. "How long has it been since you've had a weekend off?"

She shrugged. "I don't know. Years."

He nodded. "Take this one off."

Her smile was just a touch patronizing. He obviously didn't understand. "Champions don't take weekends off," she began, but he stopped the words in her throat. His hand on her hip tightened.

"Champions need to relax just like anyone else," he told her. His eyes held hers. "This champion is going to take a weekend off." His hand left its grip and began a slow journey along the rounded length of her side.

A weekend off. It had finally come through to her that he wanted to spend not only a full night, but an entire weekend with her. But she couldn't possibly do that! As Eleanor always said, every practice missed will show up in the finals.

Besides, as much as she would like to pretend this was the beginning of a beautiful relationship, she had to face the truth. She knew what he wanted. Not that he wasn't attracted to her. He wasn't faking that. But still, behind it all lay the real reason he'd come to her in the first place.

"Luke, I can't. . . ."

"You will." He said it so solemnly, as if there was nothing at all she could do about it. "I'm going to require your presence."

She shivered as his hand began to explore the slope that led to her navel. "What do you mean? What for?"

"Isn't it obvious?" He rose and let his hand slip down along the length of her leg, turning it so that the inside of her ankle was presented before him. "I need time to get to know you." His thumb began a slow circular movement across the pulse point of her ankle, now held securely in his hand.

She swallowed as her blood quickened in her veins. "How much time will you need?" she asked shakily.

"A lot of time." He leaned down and kissed the inside of her ankle, then began to explore the inner flesh of her legs with his tongue, slowly moving higher. "Days," he murmured, tickling her skin with his warm breath. "Weeks, maybe years." He nibbled sensuously on her inner thigh. "But we'll start with one long weekend."

She felt as though she were melting under his touch. She had very little will left. "I can't," she tried again, but it was painfully evident that she was making only a token effort.

"You must," he countered. "I want to know everything about you. I want to explore every inch of your body, every nuance of your soul." His kiss was sending excitement soaring through her once more. "I want to test all your responses and unravel all your secrets."

"Oh!" She writhed away from his touch. "I don't have any secrets."

He smiled. "Of course you have secrets. Everybody does."

She shook her head emphatically. "Not me."

He took her ankle in his strong grip again. "Then it

should be easy to learn all about you." His finger traced
the edges of a silver white scar that ran from the front of
her calf back to the calf muscle. "Tell me about this for
starters. What happened?"

She half rose to look at it. She hadn't thought about it
for such a long time, it took a moment to make sure it
was the right scar, the right memory.

"I got that the summer I was fifteen." She reached
down and touched it herself, as if to make sure it was
real. "I made a bad move on a reverse pike dive and hit
a cement platform."

He swore softly, covering the scar with his hand as
though to take away the pain of long ago. "You didn't
break the leg?"

She shook her head. "The cut was pretty bad and the
bone was bruised." She flexed her toes experimentally,
remembering. "My parents wanted me to quit diving
after it happened."

He looked searchingly at her. "I don't blame them,"
he said gruffly.

Leaning back, she unconsciously fingered the ace of
diamonds at her neck. "They thought it was all foolish-
ness, anyway. They didn't understand that it was everything to me." Her voice grew faint. "That I was nothing
without it."

Luke moved impatiently and she hurried on, not
wanting to get caught up in an argument about that. "It
gave them a good excuse to get me out. But I had a fairy
godperson." She grinned. "At least that was what he
seemed like. My Uncle Max. He came to the rescue."

Luke was very quiet, waiting to hear the rest.

"My father wanted to expand his furniture store. He
couldn't get a loan from the bank. He asked Max, but
Max said he didn't think it would be a good investment,
considering there was a lot of competition." She sighed.

"Poor daddy. Nothing ever went quite the way he wanted it to. When Max heard about them pulling me out of diving, he came by and took my father out on the town." She shook her head. "My father never—I mean never—went out on the town. They were out all night. By the time they got back my father had the money for his expansion and I was back in diving."

"Good old Uncle Max."

She nodded, smiling slightly.

"Is he the one who gave you that gold medallion?"

She looked down and found her fingers on the charm, but still she was impressed at Luke's perception. "Yes," she told him. "He gave it to me that day. I've worn it ever since. It's my good-luck charm, especially for diving."

"Good-luck charm," he murmured, his fingers lightly brushing the inside of her thigh. "That's what I need. Will you be my good-luck charm?"

She giggled, moving a bit nervously. "You think you can wear me on a chain around your neck?" she asked.

"No," he growled, taking her body to him again. "But there are other ways." His mouth came to hers in open invitation, his tongue flickering over her lips.

She was amazed that he could trigger the excitement again so easily. Sighing with sleepy acquiescence, she took him to her and ran her hands across the taut muscles of his back, joining him in the rhythm that they quickly revived, as though it had only been resting, waiting to be called out again.

She went with him to his hotel in the morning. He called Eleanor himself to tell her Jean would be taking the weekend off. Jean expected fireworks from her coach, but from the chuckles and light banter she heard on Luke's end of the conversation, it was evident he'd charmed Eleanor into agreeing cheerfully.

"She says I can keep you as long as I want," he told her as he hung up the phone.

She set her coffee mug down on the counter and glared at him. "Don't get any ideas," she warned.

"Ideas!" He laughed. "We've gone beyond ideas, Jean." He leaned across the counter and kissed the tip of her nose. "We're into the real stuff now."

He looked so endearing in her kitchen with the morning sunlight streaming in to burnish his hair. She had a hard time keeping herself from staring at him constantly. Everything about him seemed to fascinate her.

She packed a light overnight bag to take to his hotel, then ran around the house watering every plant before she could leave them.

"I suppose you have to talk to each one of them, too," Luke said, his eagerness to get on their way just barely concealed. "Have a little chat, find out how their day has gone."

"Of course." She flashed him a smile as she tipped her watering can in the pot for her tall ficus benjamina. Reaching in through the teardrop-shaped leaves, she took hold of the trunk and gave the little tree a hearty shake.

"Don't tell me, let me guess," Luke said wisely. "He made a pass and you're putting him in his place."

She groaned. "Hardly. I heard once that it's good for them to have a shake every day. It reminds them of a stiff breeze in the wild. They grow stronger that way."

"In the wild?" he repeated incredulously. "I've heard of going a little nuts over pet animals, but this is the first time I've seen it happen with pet plants."

She put down her watering can and faced him indignantly. "I am not going a 'little nuts.' My plants have no names. I don't let them eat at the table with me."

He rolled his eyes. "Thank heavens for that," he murmured.

"At least not when anyone's watching." She met his eyes, trying to maintain a straight face, but the crinkles at the edges of his eyes did her in and soon they were both laughing.

They rode in his long silver Mercedes to the Camelot. Jean felt as though she didn't dare touch anything for fear she would leave fingerprints.

Bobby, the valet, took the car. "Would you please bring this bag up when you have a chance?" Luke asked him.

At first Jean thought it a bit silly. She was certainly capable of carrying the small bag herself. But as she walked through the lobby of the sumptuous hotel, she was very glad she didn't have a little carrying case in her hands, signaling exactly what she was doing there.

Things were bad enough without it. Luke held his arm around her protectively, but she was sure everyone was looking at her, pointing out that she looked like an interloper, that her slacks must have come from the local army surplus and her blouse from a desert trading post.

Funny how it hadn't bothered her the other night when they'd come here for dinner. She'd been proud and not ready to accept anyone's criticism of her way of dressing and lack of money. But that was days ago, light-years ago. Things were different now.

"I can guess what she's here for, can't you?" she imagined them saying behind raised hands, snickering. She didn't belong here and it was obvious. There was only one thing that would bring her here on Luke's arm.

"I'd like the keys to the King Arthur Suite," Luke was saying to the man behind the desk. Jean kept her head high, but she imagined she could see the derision in the deskman's eyes.

"Certainly, Mr. Chisholm," was what he said, but she thought she could hear the rest with her mind's ear. *So he's got a new one, has he? Not as pretty as most of his girls are. Wonder what her hidden talent is?*

She flushed with hot embarrassment as they walked toward the elevator. "What is it?" Luke asked her, suddenly concerned. "Are you all right? Your face is positively scarlet."

It was on the tip of her tongue to answer, "What else would a scarlet woman be?" but luckily she held it back and merely shook her head.

Grow up, Jean, she told herself fiercely. *The rest of the world thinks nothing of this sort of thing. Nobody cares. It happens every day, to everybody.*

But not to me, something inside answered. No, she couldn't take it that lightly. This was special. She wouldn't have done this with any other man.

9

THEY TOOK THE ELEVATOR to the top of the tower. The doors opened onto a sunlit court planted with greenery under a glass skylight. Four doors led into four different suites, each taking up a separate corner of the top of the building.

The King Arthur Suite was gigantic. "You could hold a royal coronation in here," Jean exclaimed, "with room left over for some jousting. How positively decadent!"

"Right," he agreed happily. "Great, isn't it?"

She stood in the middle of the sitting-room area and turned slowly, gazing at the fine tapestry upholstery, the curved-legged antiques. She felt very small and insignificant. "Do you really stay in a place like this whenever you come here?" she asked.

He laughed, stepping forward to sweep her up into his arms. "Don't be ridiculous," he answered. "All I need is a bed and a bathroom ordinarily. I took this suite just for you, for this weekend." He planted a kiss on her lips. "No one is to know we're here, not even Sheila and Danni. I've told the desk to hold all calls."

Jean joined in the laughter, wrapping her arms around his neck and hugging him tightly. Somehow knowing he'd taken this set of rooms just for their time together made it much more comfortable here. It was a retreat for both of them, not a castle he'd let her enter for a brief visit.

"Come take a look." He put her back on her feet and

led her out through the formal dining room and onto the terrace. A wrought-iron railing held them back from the edge and lush greenery lined the boundaries. In the center of the terrace a small swimming pool sparkled in the morning sun. Nearby, a table and two chairs looked like an inviting place to have breakfast.

"Look!" she cried, running to the railing. "You can see all of Las Vegas below."

The city stretched out before them like a jumble of steel and concrete with a few trees scattered here and there. Cars clogged the main streets. It was civilization in its most intense form. But all one had to do was lift the eyes a bit and there was the desert, stark and dry and uninhabitable, with purple mountains on the horizon.

"This is some place." She turned toward him, smiling. "Like something out of a movie. I feel like I should be dressed in ermine and pearls."

"Oh, no," he protested, moving in closer and sliding his hands up under her blouse. "You're dressed in much too much already." And he began to remedy that situation with skillful haste.

"Luke," she protested, trying to stop his hands. "Not out here."

"Why not?" His hands on her bare skin felt strong and loving. "No one can see us up here. The only thing we have to fear may be a passing helicopter, and I don't think there will be many of them flying by today."

Reluctantly she let him undress her, giggling when he tickled places she had trouble defending. Then she was pulling off his clothes too, finding what made him laugh and running when he tried to retaliate, until the two of them were rolling on the thick carpet of the sitting room, Jean squealing and Luke growling with mock menace.

A loud pounding on the door stopped them cold. For one moment they stared in one another's eyes, Luke still laughing, Jean horrified. Then she scrambled to her feet and ran for the bedroom while Luke wrapped a towel around his hips and went to answer the door.

"Thanks, Bobby," she heard him say. "No, I don't think I'll need the car again this weekend."

She stayed in the luxurious bedroom and then walked restlessly through the dressing area, which was completely lined with mirrors, and into the bathroom, which was as large as her living room at home. It had a sunken tub and towels as thick as fur coats.

"It was only Bobby," Luke said, coming into the bedroom and dropping her overnight case on the dressing table.

"Only Bobby," she muttered, mortified. "He must have heard us!"

"Of course, he heard us. He apologized for pounding on the door. Said he'd been knocking for quite some time but we didn't seem to hear him."

"Oh!" She hid her face in her hands, laughing but truly embarrassed. "What does he think of us?"

Luke grinned. "He's jealous, of course. Wishes he was the one up here with you."

She lowered her hands and stared at him. "Don't be silly," she said weakly.

"Are you kidding?" He dropped his towel and came toward her again. "You should have seen the way he was looking into the room, hoping to catch a glimpse of you." He took her in his arms. "Why is it that you can't believe what a desirable woman you are?" he asked her, bemused. "I think your years of concentration on diving have damaged some part of your brain."

He did his best for the rest of the day to prove to her that a desirable woman was exactly what she was. As

they played and sunned themselves and talked sleepily,
lying side by side, she almost came to believe it.

Luke fell asleep in the sun, but Jean was too restless.
She watched him sleep for a few minutes, enjoying the
wave of tenderness he stirred in her. Then she rose and
walked across the terrace, entering the hotel room.

Laughter bubbled in her throat. Here she was, walking around naked in a strange place, and already it felt
perfectly comfortable. She looked at the soft carpeting,
and the next thing she knew she was taking a flying leap
into the air and going into a cartwheel across the floor.

She landed in a heap, laughing out loud and looking
quickly to make sure Luke was still sleeping. If he'd seen
her...!

Luckily he was still where she'd left him. She pulled
herself up and walked into the bedroom. She might as
well take a look at herself while she had a moment
alone.

The dressing area was enclosed in mirrors and she
stood in the middle of the room, turning slowly and
examining every curve and angle.

"Not bad, Jean old girl," she decided finally, grinning
at her reflection. All these years of rigorous training had
helped keep her slim and muscular. Maybe she was as
desirable as Luke said she was.

Desirable or not, at least she had nothing to be
ashamed of. There was an extra spring in her step as she
returned to sit beside Luke in the sun.

They ordered lunch from room service and the fruit
salads came dressed up with skirts of whipped cream
and mint leaves. They took a long lazy nap on the huge
four-poster bed, then went outside for a swim in their
miniature swimming pool. The pool was no longer than
six feet by twelve and the depth was four feet at the
most.

"Not deep enough to dive in," she said as they walked down the steps and into the cool water, holding hands.

He pulled her around and stopped her speech with a quick kiss. "We're not going to mention that word all weekend," he told her firmly. "We're detached from everything else in the world."

Detached from everything else in the world. That was just the way she wanted it, too. That left her open to enjoy the man she knew she was beginning to love, open to accept his compliments and words of affection without having to let her natural skepticism go to work, destroying her joy. There were many unresolved problems between them, but if they could stay detached from the world, those problems could be ignored. At least for the weekend.

The water welcomed them and they drifted around the pool, splashing and laughing, then sitting on the submerged ledge that ran around one end of the pool, letting the water lap around their naked bodies as the sun beat down overhead.

"I'll bet the real King Arthur never had it this good," Luke murmured, slipping an arm around her shoulders and pulling her toward him through the water.

Jean almost answered with a joke about Queen Guinevere, but she stopped herself in time. After all, the Queen was married to Arthur. If she compared herself to Guinevere, what would Luke think?

"How is your knee treating you these days?" she asked instead.

"Not bad." He raised the leg in the water and let her see his limited flexion. "Could be better." His smile was wistful. "You don't realize when you're young that the injuries you sustain will be with you all your life. Oh that I'd had the wisdom at twenty-one that I have at thirty-six."

She sighed in sympathetic agreement. "People do tend to think their bodies will last forever and do anything. Though I must say, some overdo it a bit more than others," she added. "If you'd had a little more sense...."

"You're absolutely right. I won't deny it. I stayed in football long after I should have bowed out."

Jean felt a warning prickle along the back of her neck. Something told her there was a reason he was saying this.

"I loved football," he went on as though he didn't notice she was stiffening beside him. "I lived for the game. I loved the rush of excitement when we ran out onto the field, the contact, the bands. And the victory." He shook his head, remembering. "There's nothing like the victories, is there?"

He was quiet for a long moment but she knew there was more coming. Finally he spoke again.

"That's why I stayed in that last year. I couldn't bear to think of letting all that go. So, even though my knee was badly injured, I stayed in, playing with my knee taped and shot full of painkiller." He grimaced. "I didn't do myself or my teammates a favor by doing it. I played lousy football. I should've known it was time to make way for a younger player."

Now he was coming awfully close to home. She clenched her hands into fists, her nails digging into her flesh. *Change the subject*, she begged silently. *Don't do this.*

"Top athletes are basically very selfish people," he went on softly. "They have to be. Everything they do, everything everyone around them does, is all geared toward being the best." He sighed, started to say something more, then seemed to stop himself.

He was saying that she was a selfish person, that

hanging onto her championship was not only fool-
hardy, it was greedy and stupid. She couldn't look at
him, she couldn't speak to him. Instead she turned
away, slipped into the water and sank from sight.

Back and forth she went like a pacing dolphin under
the water, swimming as hard as she could, not even
needing to come up for air. She resented what he'd said,
but it scared her as well. There'd been pieces of truth in
everything he brought up. She couldn't deny that. She
just wasn't sure she could deal with it.

She felt rather than saw his body split the water, and
then he was swimming beside her, his hands running
along the muscles of her back, urging her to come up to
the surface. She came, gasping for breath, and he stood
back watching her until she regained control.

She looked at him with the water streaming in silver
rivulets down his tan skin and she knew she didn't want
the day to end like this. If only he would put reality
back out the door, so would she.

"You would've made a good King Arthur," she told
him breathlessly. "You have a heroic air about you."

The hard look in his eyes melted and he gave her a
half grin, but he didn't say anything. He just looked at
her and something in his gaze was disconcerting. She
kicked off from the bottom again, but this time it was to
arch back and let her body float in the golden sunshine,
narrowing her eyes until they were only slits of dazzling
light as the sun cast its spell on the drops on her lashes.

She was floating on her back with her body just
below the surface of the water, but Luke was standing
waist deep beside her. She could see his hair shining, his
shoulders wide and dark, his eyes as brilliant as the sun
itself.

Suddenly she felt his hand in the small of her back,
gently coaxing her body to move higher in the water.

The desert breeze felt cool on her nipples as they broke the surface and then tightened into hard dark peaks. The palm of his hand soon covered one, then the other, barely touching them at first, then massaging them gently as though to make them relax again, while his other hand still held her high in the water.

Jean opened her eyes as the electricity began to hum through her veins again, but he shook his head, showing her with his touch that he wanted her to stay as she was. She closed her eyes again, arching back and letting his hand begin a slow exploration of the valley between her breasts, the dip between her ribs, the rounded mound of her navel, and then lower with a flicker of hungry fire that made her gasp and shoot upright again.

"Can't you float any longer?" he asked as though disappointed.

"Not when you're doing that," she said, throwing back her wet hair.

His smile was slow and seductive. "Then we'll just have to do something else."

He curled an arm around her and pulled her toward the steps, depositing her on the middle one so that she sat submerged above her waist, her breasts swaying on the water. She looked up as he stood above her and he seemed so dark, so large, that he blotted out the sun.

"King Arthur," she whispered again for some irrational reason.

"Water princess," he called her in return. "When I see you dive or swim, I can really believe you should reign over everything in the water."

She smiled, lying back against the next step in a pose she knew was provocative. "And what, pray tell, is King Arthur doing messing around with a water princess?" she asked, one eyebrow raised.

"Are you kidding?" He came down beside her, scooping up one of her breasts with his hand. "King Arthur is mad about water princesses." He leaned down to take the tip gently in his mouth, tugging on it while his other hand went to the small of her back working small urgent circles in the flesh.

Jean felt a moan rising in her throat and moved convulsively, reaching out to put a cool hand on his hot skin. "What does Queen Guinevere have to say about that?" she managed to ask.

"Guinevere!" He raised his head and gave her a mock glare. "She ran off with Lancelot a long time ago." He kissed the open mouth she presented to him with her head thrown back. His tongue slid along the smooth surface of her teeth, then filled her mouth with evidence of his growing desire.

"Forget about Guinevere," he murmured against her lips. "She's been gone a long time and King Arthur is a lonely man. A water princess would suit him fine."

He began to lever himself on top of her but she slipped out of his grasp and moved further away on the step. "That's all very well for King Arthur," she said recklessly. "But what about the water princess? How do we know what will suit her?"

"Oh, darling," he growled, moving in to corner her against the side. His mouth went directly to the hollow at her throat while his hand spread across her skin and dove to find her most sensitive spot. "The king will suit her or die trying."

She laughed softly, not really evading him but making him work for what he got. "A bit of noblesse oblige, is it?" she teased. "The lord of the manor gets what he wants, regardless?"

His body slid along hers in the water, making her startlingly aware of the crisp ripeness of his arousal.

"The lord of the manor is your slave," he whispered huskily. "You ought to have guessed that by now."

Something about the intensity in his eyes made her wary and she tried to pull away from him again.

"No, you don't." Her friendly bantering Luke had turned into something else. She could see that drawing away was a mistake. Something beat behind his eyes, something as wild and primitive as the arid landscape on the horizon behind them.

"The game is over, Jean," he said roughly. "It's too late to hold anything back."

Her heart was racing so loudly she could hardly hear his words. "Luke," she began, a bit frightened by his ardor.

"Don't worry, darling," he told her hoarsely, his hunger just barely leashed. "I would never, never hurt you."

They came together in the shallow water and she cried out as she felt his shuddering thrust and then she joined him as his strong hands guided her into the rhythm, splashing again and again into the water, sailing above him like a bird in flight.

"I love you," she murmured as they lay back in the water together, the tiny waves created by their lovemaking still lapping around them. She said it less through bravery than because she was so deliciously tired she didn't know what she was saying. But Luke heard it and he drew her closer, though he didn't answer.

They lay together for a long time, drifting in happy oblivion. Finally the water began to feel a little cold and they retreated into the bath to wash each other's hair and prepare for dinner.

"I'm going to take you down to a real meal," Luke told her. "No room service."

"I don't have anything to wear," she protested.

"No problem." He picked up the telephone and called one of the dress shops on the main floor. "Send up a dress, size—oh, I'd say about a seven. Something sexy."

She tried to keep from smiling. "You're a pretty good size estimator."

He made a face. "What do you want me to say? That I've had plenty of practice? Forget it. I'm just naturally good at most things I try." He forced her back against the bed and kissed her soundly. "Wouldn't you agree to that?"

"You won't get an argument out of me," she admitted, chuckling. But a few minutes later she was looking at him speculatively. "Why is it that you never married?" she asked, hoping she wasn't treading on forbidden ground.

He was dressing in dinner clothes while she sat cross-legged on the bed and watched him. He looked stunningly handsome in his white shirt with the black bow tie.

He turned when she asked the question. "I never wanted to," he said simply.

She licked her lips. "Never? Not one of those lovely ladies who used to follow you around when you played football?"

"Not one," he said, tilting his head to look at her. "For a few years it was like living in a candy shop. I could hardly even tell the flavors apart. But then for some reason I lost my sweet tooth." He shrugged. "I get along all right on my own."

She wasn't sure why she'd asked that question. It wasn't as though she expected anything like that from him. Or even wanted it, she reminded herself quickly. She was a diver. Divers needed dedicated spouses just like doctors did. She knew Luke wasn't the sort to take a back seat to any career.

A knock on the door signaled the arrival of the dress

and for the next half hour they had a good laugh over it, pulling it here, pinning it there, until it looked terrific on her.

It was a simple black velvet with tiny straps and a very low neckline, and Jean loved it at first sight. Once they had it fixed right, Luke said, "You've got to wear your hair up with this."

Jean was stricken. "I never wear my hair up," she wailed.

He nodded. "You must. And you need earrings, the kind that dangle almost to your shoulders."

A quick call to the lobby jewelry shop produced a set of diamond earrings that swung, while not quite to her shoulders, nicely enough to catch every bit of light and send it back with shooting sparks.

"You're not actually buying all this?" Jean asked in horror when she saw a price tag.

"The dress is yours," he said firmly.. "The earrings go back in the morning. The jeweler is a friend of mine and understands."

She tried to pin her hair up but the results were lop-sided and messy. Luke walked into the dressing room while she was trying to rectify a mistake in the back and he laughed aloud at the picture she made.

"You look like Harpo after a bad night," he chuckled.

Stung, she swung toward him. "Let's see if you can do any better," she challenged. "After all, this was your idea."

"Me?" he cried, as though she'd asked him to dress in drag.

"Why not you? I thought you were so good at every-thing you tried."

He narrowed his eyes, looking at her with reluctant interest. "It shouldn't be too difficult," he conceded. "But you can't look until I'm finished."

She sat still while his quick hands worked on her hair. An awkward apprehension began to grip her. Heaven only knew what terrible thing he could do to her. Would she have to wear it, regardless? She began to wish she'd watched her tongue.

A nervous silence reigned, punctuated now and then by small cries of pain as he jabbed the pins into her scalp.

"Sorry," he muttered for the tenth time, and then he turned her in the chair so that she could see herself.

Her jaw dropped. He'd done a marvelous job and transformed her into a turn-of-the-century Gibson girl. She looked almost gorgeous.

"Wow," she murmured, glancing into the mirror at his smug smile. "What are you, a hairdresser going incognito?"

He tried to look modest and failed miserably. "Just another one of my hidden talents," he sighed. "Can I help it if I'm wonderful?"

She snorted. "Wonderfully conceited, that I'll grant you."

"Is that right?" He picked her up and raised her high. "I've got a good mind to make you eat those words."

"Luke," she cried, "put me down!"

"On the bed?" he asked hopefully. "Let's. We'll mess up your hair and then I'll have the fun of fixing it for you again."

"Anything but that," she moaned. "I'll be dripping blood across the floor if you stick me one more time with those awful hairpins."

He made a face, but he lowered her. "Genius is seldom rewarded in one's lifetime," he complained. "They never appreciate you till you're gone."

"I appreciate you." In a sudden burst of uninhibited affection, she threw her arms around his neck and kissed him hard on the mouth. "I appreciate you," she said in a ragged whisper that really said *I love you*.

His gaze clouded as he looked down into her eyes. Instead of answering, he began fumbling with the clasp on her gold chain.

"What are you doing?" she asked, reaching back to stop him.

"The chain doesn't go with the earrings," he said, but she could tell there was more to it.

"I don't care about that," she told him. "I'll wear it anyway."

He continued to try the clasp until the chain fell away into his hand. "Why not let it stay here?" he suggested. "It's for diving luck. You're not diving now. And there's a necklace that goes with the earrings for you to wear to dinner."

Reluctantly she agreed. After all, they'd made a bargain to leave other worlds out of this weekend. She might as well let the medallion join the other remnants of that life. She watched him toss it on the dressing table. It looked simple and forlorn, out of place in this lavish setting. She touched the swaying diamonds at her ears.

"Come on, water princess." He pulled her to her feet. "For some strange reason, I'm starving." He nuzzled below her ear as he fastened the diamond necklace around her throat. "If we don't get something to eat soon, I just might lose control and take a bite out of your lovely neck."

Their evening trip through the lobby was quite different from the morning one. This time Jean felt like the princess Luke was calling her. She saw people turn to watch the two of them pass, smiling in a way that showed what a nice-looking couple they made. She raised her chin and enjoyed it.

They decided to eat in the dark Pendragon's Tomb. "There's no point in being too public," Luke declared. "If Sheila and Danni catch sight of us we'll never get rid of them."

That prospect was enough to convince Jean. She certainly wanted to stay away from the two of them. As they walked down the long hallway lined with exclusive shops, she couldn't help but wonder what would happen if they did run into the Worths. Would Sheila try to take Luke back?

Her jaw hardened at the thought. *Let her try,* she thought fiercely. *Just let her try.*

At that moment she caught sight of her own reflection in a mirror and almost laughed aloud. *What a toughie,* she chided herself silently. *Wow, Sheila better watch her step.*

Pendragon's Tomb was as spooky as ever. "They really should provide flashlights," she whispered to Luke as they groped their way to their table. "I wonder if they've ever been sued by an accident-prone patron?"

"Impossible," he replied, helping her into her seat. "The process server could never find anyone to hand the warrant to in here."

The menu consisted of cornish game hen stuffed with truffles and garnished with wild rice. They both ate enough for a small army and Luke ordered dessert, as well.

"We have chocolate mousse tonight, sir," the waiter told him.

"That will do fine. And bring along a mint liqueur to go with it, as well as coffee."

"Oh, no," Jean groaned. "I'll never find room for all that."

"Yes, you will," he argued confidently. "I have a lot of faith in your stamina."

It felt so comfortable being here with him. She remembered the night they'd come before, how thrilled she'd been, how scared. She wasn't scared anymore. She knew what the stakes were. But she faced them unafraid. She'd face anything for this time with Luke.

Jean smiled to herself, thinking how Luke had asked Jeffrey his intentions regarding her then. Luke had worn quite a grin on his face when she informed him earlier that Jeffrey was now engaged to someone.

Suddenly she remembered Uncle Max and the birthday dinner at the Golden Palace. "Reach for the stars, Jean," he'd urged her. "You'll never get more than you try for. And if you don't try, you'll never know how far you might have gone."

He'd been the driving force behind her involvement in serious diving. Her parents had been heartily against it.

"We're not that sort, Jean," her father would tell her, shaking his head sadly. "We've all got to face our limits. Not like your Uncle Max." He would wince as he said the name. "He's flying high now, but you mark my words, girl. What goes up must come down."

What goes up must come down. She smiled sadly as she thought of the words. She'd gone so high, jumping into space, out where she was so very vulnerable, trying for as much beauty as she could grasp. And she knew each time she had to come down. But the flight was so fine, so free. It was worth the landing.

"What are you thinking about?" Luke asked her softly. "Whatever it is brings such a shine to your eyes they look like stars in a midnight sky."

She reached to touch his cheek. "I'm thinking about freedom," she told him gently. "About taking risks and paying the price."

He stared at her for a long time, holding her hand to

his cheek with his own fingers. "What price are you willing to pay, Jean?" he asked.

She stared back, wondering just what he meant. A chill sent a spiny finger down her back and she shivered, looking away and casting about for some way to change the subject.

She looked at the light dessert the waiter had set before her. "A thickening waistline, probably, if I eat all this mousse," she said, looking up to see if he was willing to let it go at that.

She could see the rebellion in his eyes, but then he seemed to think better of pursuing something she wanted to avoid.

"Eat it," he advised casually. "Damn the consequences."

She took a huge bite and savored it. "Do you suppose these people realize they're in the presence of King Arthur himself?" she teased him a moment later.

"Let's hope not," he returned. "Someone's sure to have a sword stuck in stone he'd want me to pull out."

She giggled. "Does that happen to you a lot?" she asked sympathetically.

He nodded gloomily. "All the time. Not only do I have bad knees, I'm beginning to develop sword elbow."

She groaned. "I can tell you've already contracted a fatal dose of bad-joke-itis."

They wandered around the casino floor before going back up to the room. Luke walked with his arm around her and she felt a peaceful joy she'd never known before in the shelter of his embrace. They wandered by the roped-off areas where well-dressed men put down hundreds of dollars on a silly looking game in which cards were dealt by a plastic box, then past the craps and poker tables. Suddenly Jean saw a face she thought she recognized.

She had to stop and look again. The woman was dressed in a top hat and a very skimpy dress made to look like a caricature of a man's tuxedo. The makeup was awfully heavy, but beneath the mascara and false eyelashes, Jean was sure she saw her friend Bette Random.

"It's Bette," she said in amazement. Luke turned to look at her too.

"Your friend from the Department of Sports Medicine?"

"Yes. What on earth is she doing here?" Knowing how Bette felt about gambling, Jean wanted to back away and pretend she hadn't seen this. It was as though this was something she knew Bette would just as soon hide.

But that was impossible, of course. "Can you wait for just a minute?" she asked Luke, who readily agreed. Resolutely she stepped forward and sat on a stool at the blackjack table where Bette was dealing.

"Hi, there," she said with forced cheer. "Can we talk?"

Bette looked at her and then quickly away again. Jean watched as her friend bit her lip, looking down at her hands. Turning, Bette signaled to the pit boss.

"I need a five-minute break. Okay?"

The man looked none too pleased, but he nodded and Bette came away with Jean.

"I'm not supposed to talk to customers on the floor, you know," she said nervously, looking around. "So we've got to make this fast."

Jean came very close. "What on earth are you doing here?" she hissed. "I can't believe it! Did you quit at the university or what?"

"No." Bette lifted her head and glared at Jean. "No, I didn't quit. But just how did you think I was going to afford to pay for daily physical therapy for Andy on my salary at the university?"

Of course. Why hadn't she thought about it at all? She'd known there was no insurance money, but it hadn't occurred to her that Bette might be unable to pay.

"But Bette, dealing again, when you've had such strong convictions against it."

Bette's face looked cold. It was partly the makeup, but there was more to it than that and Jean had a sudden fear of losing a very good friend.

"My convictions don't mean much when my child is lying there, unable to walk properly and in pain," she said harshly. "I'd do anything to get him well again. anything."

She twisted away from the hand Jean tried to put on her arm and went back to her table. Jean watched her go, feeling as though a new side of her friend had opened up to her. Or maybe it was just a side of the world she'd ignored up to now.

Luke's arms slid around her from behind. "You all right?" he asked softly.

She nodded, turning back to give him a smile. "I'm fine." She wanted him to hold her tightly but she didn't feel quite free enough to ask for that. Besides, she stood on her own two feet, didn't she?

It wasn't until much later when they were sitting at the edge of their pool trailing their bare feet in the water and looking up at the star-studded sky that she told him all about Bette and her problem.

"How much does she need?" he asked right away. "I'll take care of it."

She stared at him. The contrast between having so much money one threw it around on fancy suites like this one and having to give up one's principles just to make ends meet was cruelly vivid.

Not that she resented Luke's affluence. He'd worked hard for it. From the stories he'd told her tonight, she knew about his poverty-stricken childhood in a little town in Texas.

"Deadwood was the official name," he'd told her. "But they might as well have just named it Death. Nothing seemed to thrive there."

Nothing but Luke Chisholm. He told her about his rise through athletic ability. It took a lot of hard physical work to hone that ability into something special, and all the time he'd known his life at the top wouldn't last long, and he'd prepared himself, working part-time, then taking over at low-level jobs until he'd proved his worth.

"I sold insurance, stocks and bonds, athletic supplies; you name it, I've probably hawked it somewhere. I worked on commissions," he told her. "That means you can either work your tail off and, if you're good, make a lot of money, or you can lie around and feel sorry for yourself until you starve to death."

He'd worked his tail off, living frugally until he'd saved enough to start his own company in San Francisco. Brock Worth had come in with him and they'd been business partners as well as best friends.

"We started out making footballs," he'd told her. "That was, after all, where our hearts lay. But we had success right from the start and quickly expanded to cover all sorts of athletic equipment." He stretched with lazy pride. "And now we're a major corporation with holdings all over the place." He grinned. "Things that have nothing to do with football. I even have a piece of a movie studio."

He'd worked hard for his wealth. But it was his, not hers, and Bette was her friend.

"Just let me know what Bette needs and I'll give you a check for her," he said again.

She reached out and traced the crease along his cheek with a gentle finger. "No," she whispered. "She'd never accept it."

"Why not?" He took her hand and kissed the fingers, looking searchingly into her eyes. "I've got the money, she doesn't. I can't think of a better use for it."

Her smile was melancholy. "Would you have accepted that sort of gift from a stranger when you were poor?" she asked.

He frowned. "No, but then I was stupid and proud. . . ."

"And so is Bette." She kissed him lightly. "I'll have to think of another way."

They talked no more about it, but Jean couldn't get Bette's problem out of her mind. Long after Luke fell asleep in the huge bed, she lay awake staring at the ceiling. Just a week before her life had been traveling along the orderly path she'd set it on. The most major problem had been getting enough time to fit her classes in between the training for the World Games. Now everything had turned around.

It was as though she'd lived safe and secure in a desert surrounded by beautiful polished stones for a long time, and then one day she'd begun to turn them over, one by one. The other side of each stone revealed cracks and spiders and lizards, things she'd never dreamed existed there.

Her safe secure life had evaporated, and in its place were questions and puzzles that needed answers, decisions to be made, steps to be taken, and most of all, truths to be faced.

She rose on one elbow and looked at the man sleeping beside her. He looked young and innocent, but hardly vulnerable. There was a basic toughness about him, a steely strength that held true even in sleep.

Softly she pushed back a lock of hair that had strayed

over his forehead. She loved him so much, her heart seemed to swell in her chest and tears rushed, stinging, to her eyes. Luke had been the first person to make her face the possibility of life without diving, and at the same time he was the only one who'd ever touched her the way diving did.

It wasn't as if this was a choice between Luke and diving. If that were the case, her agony might be even worse. No, Luke was attracted to her, but his main objective was still to sign her up as Danni's coach. She had no illusions on that score.

Silently she slipped from the bed and reached for her clothes, putting them on with reluctant determination. Luke moved once, turning on his side and stretching out his arm as though to find her, but he fell back into a deeper sleep as she watched, and she left the room, moving quietly through the shadows across the heavily carpeted floor toward the door.

10

JEAN LEFT HER OVERNIGHT BAG behind. She could get it later, and she would feel a little conspicuous walking through the hotel carrying it now. The elevator took her down to the main floor and she stepped out into the high-ceilinged room.

Though it was three in the morning, the casino floor was as busy as it had been at noon. Lights flashed, voices echoed, coins jangled and for a moment, the room seemed to swirl around her in a dizzying maelstrom.

She soon got her bearings. Slowly she began to wander through the banks of silver slot machines, listening to the sound of humanity all around her.

A whirring siren caught her attention and she stopped to watch a laughing husband-and-wife team gather the steady stream of silver dollars that poured from their machine. Winners.

Looking around at the envious faces watching along with her, she wondered how many of them would win tonight and how many would go to their rooms with their hopes unfulfilled.

Only the lucky ones, she thought sadly. Only the few lucky ones would ever have their heart's desire. The rest would go through life without it.

She closed her eyes and steadied herself. *Come on, Jean,* she told herself angrily. *Don't be such a drip. Look around. The winners are happy, but so are the others. They go on. They still hope.*

Suddenly she couldn't stand the noise and color and confusion. She hurried outside and hailed a cab to drive her home. The neon lights shining against the sky seemed strangely mocking to her now. She was glad to get back on the quiet residential street where her apartment building was.

Once home, she changed into jeans and a work shirt and went to get her car from the garage. If she hurried she could be so far out on the desert by sunrise, she'd be able to enjoy it without having to see any sign of the city.

She pulled onto the highway, racing along the silver ribbon that tied the city to the wilderness. Every now and then she passed a car heading into Las Vegas, but she saw no one else going in her direction.

She found the side road she was looking for and turned down it, away from the highway. Now she knew she would meet no one at all.

The sunrise was magnificent. She parked the car on the side of the road and walked onto the sandy waste to watch the desert change as the shadows and sunlight played their daily game of hide and seek. The sky looked like the inside of a pearly seashell, and the desert floor turned from white to purple to silver as she watched. The mountains were as black as cardboard cutout silhouettes at first, then they sprang into proper dimension as the light hit them. It was a dramatic scene, one she never tired of.

She sat so long and so quietly that tiny desert animals began to scurry around her, thinking her a part of the landscape. Beetles made their clumsy way across the sand beside her while tiny lizards darted from one rock to the next, looking for something more palatable than the huge black beetles.

But though her body was quiet, her mind was working feverishly. She'd made a major revelation and she was coming to grips with it.

She'd always been very proud of being a goal-oriented person. She firmly believed that little was accomplished unless goals were set, and she'd lived by that. Her major goal had always been the diving championship and she'd done everything, anything, to reach her goal.

Had she done too much? Had she sacrificed a normal life and the relationships around her just to succeed? Had she been right to disregard her father's warnings, her mother's fears? The criticisms of her friends and lovers?

She'd thought so at the time. She knew there was no other way to become, and then to stay, champion. It was the most important thing in the world to her. Was that wrong?

She closed her eyes and rocked slowly back and forth. People were the most important things. Relationships. Trust and generosity and caring. But where did those things fit in with her goals?

She loved Luke more than anyone, anything. But what would she give up to have him? Would any price be too steep?

She rose and paced across the sand. Why would Luke want her? Why would he want a woman who had no room in her life for anything but her own ambitions?

Luke had implied she was selfish and he was right. All her life she'd worked so hard to become a champion, she'd allowed others to support her without ever realizing or appreciating how much they'd done for her. She'd taken so much from others, and what had she ever given back?

It was time to give something back. She wasn't worthy of Luke's love, of anyone's love, the way she was. She couldn't give up her goals. They were too much a part of her. But she could do something about changing the way she went about achieving them.

The sun was high and hot by the time she climbed back in her car and turned it toward the city. She'd made some hard decisions, but just in the making of them she felt lighter and freer than she'd felt for days.

Her first stop in Las Vegas was at Eleanor and Mike's little cottage behind the nursery he was developing for his landscaping business. She walked through the rolls of sod and rows of eucalyptus trees to get to their front door.

"Hi," she called to Mike.

He was building wooden lathing for his roses. When he heard her voice he stood up, his spare frame reaching well over six feet, and watched her walk for a moment before greeting her.

"Hi, yourself. How's it going?" He shifted his weight uncomfortably and Jean knew Eleanor must have told him that they'd discussed his wanting her to quit coaching. "Eleanor's in the kitchen."

Jean grinned, unable to resist ribbing him. "Where you like her, huh?"

He frowned, stepping toward her. "No, you don't understand, it's not like that at all. . . ."

She laughed, heading for the kitchen. "I know. You two want to build a life together. I'm only kidding." She made a face at him before she entered the house. "Don't take life so seriously. It's fatal. Believe me, I know."

Eleanor was washing dishes and Jean wasted no time on preliminaries. "We're going to cut down on training," she told her firmly. "We'll continue with the mornings, but in the afternoons I'll be busy doing something else."

Eleanor's eyes widened in horror.

"I know you think there's no chance that way, but I've decided to withdraw from the platform competition. I only had a marginal chance there, anyway. We'll concentrate on springboard."

Eleanor was shaking her head. "You'll never make it with half-hearted training," she began angrily, but Jean cut in again.

"I'll make it. Believe me, I still intend to win." She sighed. "Don't you see? This will give you more time to work with Mike, to start knitting little booties and things like that."

Eleanor came toward her. "Jean, you can't do this. I know how much it means to you, and if I can't cut it you'll just have to find another coach. . . ."

"No." Jean smiled with easy confidence. "We'll do it. You just wait and see."

She knew Eleanor thought her new plan had something to do with Luke but she didn't bother to disabuse her of the notion. She'd find out soon enough.

Her next stop was at Bette's. She found her friend out in the backyard pulling oxalis out of her carefully nurtured dichondra lawn. Andy was on the sidelines reading to her while she worked.

"What are you reading?" Jean asked Andy, not yet ready to look Bette in the eye.

"Tom Sawyer," he replied. He was a solid chunk of a kid with a shock of red hair and freckles everywhere. "We've got to read it for English and mom says she likes to hear it while she works, so we're killing two birds with one stone." He grinned at her.

Jean looked at Bette whose head was bent over her weeding. She hadn't said a word beyond the original greeting. Behind her, on the clothesline, she saw the uniform Bette had been wearing the night before. Without a warning she walked quickly to the line and pulled down the skimpy piece of clothing.

"What are you doing?" Bette sounded only curious at first, but when she saw Jean march to the trash can and throw the uniform in, she was shocked. "Jean," she cried, rising from her knees, "what right do you have to make judgments?"

"Bette, Bette." She ran to her friend and threw her arms around her. "I'm not making judgments. But you said you were only dealing in order to pay for Andy's physical therapy, right?"

Bette nodded, her face wooden, her eyes confused.

"Well, you won't have to pay for that any longer. I'm going to do it."

Bette shook her head, uncomprehending. "How could you possibly? He needs daily care. . . . "

Jean hugged her friend. "I know. I know all about it, remember? I'm cutting down on training. My afternoons will be free to research better ways of therapy for Andy, and then we'll spend a lot of time together, he and I." She turned to smile back at the boy. "Mostly swimming. Would you like that?"

"Would I!"

Bette was shaking her head. "I can't let you do that. It's not right. You want that championship so much."

Jean nodded. "Yes, but that's not all I want. Your happiness and welfare mean a lot to me. More than I let myself realize." She held Bette tightly and closed her eyes. "You've got to let me do this, Bette. Please. I'm begging you."

"Yeah," Andy's reedy voice piped in. "I'm begging you too!"

They both laughed, and then they were crying and laughing and holding each other as though a strong wind might be along soon to blow one of them away.

It was going to be all right. Together they could accomplish miracles.

The last stop promised to be the most difficult. She pulled into the parking lot at the Camelot, resisting the impulse to pull her dusty Mustang up in front for the valet to park. Instead she went to the visitor's parking lot and ran in through a side entrance. Today she was dressed like a careless teenager in jeans and an old shirt, but she didn't waste a thought on how she appeared to others as she had the day before. She had more important things on her mind.

She'd been dreading returning to the room where she and Luke had spent such a wonderful day, so she was relieved when she ran into him in the lobby.

"Where the hell have you been?" came thundering out of his mouth before she had a chance to say a word. "I've turned this town upside down all day looking for you!"

"We've got to talk," she said, unconsciously backing away as he came toward her.

He nodded curtly and gestured toward the elevator. "Let's go."

"No." She took a deep breath because it was hard to go against him and she knew she was going to be doing a lot of it in the next few minutes. "In the bar."

He looked as though he were about to pick her up bodily and carry her up to the room, but he controlled himself and nodded. "Okay. Lead the way."

She turned into a dark cavernlike room beside the casino. Merlin's Cave, it said at the entrance. Inside the walls glowed with psychedelic colors and jagged artificial stalactites filled with more colored lights hung from the ceiling.

They found a secluded booth and sat across from one another. Luke's face was angry and she didn't blame him, but it still cut sharply into her soul.

They ordered drinks from the waitress and when she left their table, Luke leaned forward.

"Do I get an explanation of why you ran out on me in the middle of the night?" he asked coldly.

"I'm . . . I'm sorry about that. I just had to get away."

"From me?" His outrage burned in his eyes.

She ached to comfort him, but she didn't know how she could do that and still go through with this. "No. Just to have space to think."

"Oh?" His anger dimmed and he looked at her with interest. "What were you thinking about?"

She wet her lips with a nervous tongue. "I think you can guess." Raising her face to his, she steeled herself. "You've opened my eyes to a lot of things in the short time we've known each other. I've decided to make some changes in my life."

A smile began to tug at the corners of his mouth, and to her surprise that hurt even more than the anger. He thought he'd won. He thought she'd finally seen the light, that he'd persuaded her. Was that really all he cared about?

"You're going to coach Danni?" he asked hopefully.

She stared into his crystal eyes for a long moment before she shook her head. "No. I'm not. I'm a diver, not a coach. Why can't you believe that?"

Their drinks arrived and they were silent while the waitress put the ginger ale in front of Jean, the mixed drink in front of Luke. When Jean looked up at her companion she could see that his face had hardened again.

"If you can dive," he said harshly, "you can coach."

"Not necessarily. Coaching's not a bit like diving."

"Right," he said, the bitterness clear in his voice. "When you're coaching, you're not a star."

The barb hit the target and she winced. He might be saying it merely in anger, but there was a measure of truth to the words. "That might be part of it," she admitted. "But there's more."

He leaned forward and covered her hand with his own as though to make up for what he'd said. "Then don't coach Danni," he urged with smooth persuasion. "Come with me instead."

"With you?" She was startled, not really sure he meant what the words said.

"Yes. With me." He searched her eyes. "I've never known a woman quite like you, Jean. I want you in my life."

That hit her like a bombshell. It could easily have splintered all her hard-won intentions, but she braced herself, smothering the surge of joy before too much damage could be done. It could never work. Not this way. To kid herself into believing it might would only bring them both more agony in the end.

"I'm a diver," she repeated woodenly.

"You're a woman," he said, his voice very close to a snarl. His fingers tightened around hers painfully. "You want me as much as I want you. I know you do."

Her breath was coming very fast and she wanted to hurry before she lost the ability to finish this rationally. She opened her mouth to tell him goodbye, but to her amazement something else came out.

"I could easily fall in love with you," she said, then winced at her own audacity. Surprise made him loosen his grip on her hand and she quickly slipped it away. "I think you know that. I . . . I can't help my emotions."

She looked down at the table, drawing in a shuddering breath. "But I've got to defend my championship," she said, shakily before he could respond. "My whole life is aimed at this. I can't abandon a lifetime of work. You called me selfish last night and you were right. I'm too selfish for love."

She rose while he stared at her with incredulous eyes. "I just wanted to say goodbye. And to thank you for making me look at my life." She gazed at him hard as though to take a mental picture she would always cherish.

"Goodbye," she whispered. Whirling, she ran from the bar, ran from Luke and from love and from happiness.

Somehow she made it home, though she could never remember later having driven the strip of road that led to her apartment. Afraid he might try to contact her, she took her phone off the hook and left her lights off long after darkness fell that night. But no one came to her door, and as she cried herself to sleep, she chided herself for thinking he would care that much.

He knew she wouldn't withdraw from diving. He wanted a woman who had time to devote to loving him. He certainly didn't want a diver. He'd given up on her.

That was just what she wanted, wasn't it? Of course. She'd told him so herself. Then why did she feel as though she were moving in a black hole of misery?

He had her things sent over by messenger. When she opened the door to the man and saw her bag in the stranger's hand, she felt a burning lump clogging her throat. It wasn't until then that she realized she'd still harbored a tiny hope he would bring it back himself.

The black velvet dress was with her bag in a special carrier of its own. But her chain with the ace of diamonds medallion was nowhere to be found.

She agonized over that, wondering if she should call him or go over to retrieve her good-luck charm. At last she decided to ignore it. She wasn't strong enough to go to him for it. And she'd turned over a new leaf, after all. Maybe she didn't need things like good-luck charms any longer.

The roses were another matter. The first eight he'd sent her still sat in the vase looking older, but not a bit wilted. She stared at them for a long time, half wanting to throw them away, half wanting to keep them fresh forever.

Finally she shrugged. "They're just flowers, aren't they?" she asked herself. "I love flowers. I'll keep them until they wilt, then I'll throw them out. Just as I would with any bouquet."

Then she walked into her living room and saw the four roses he'd brought the night they'd first made love. He'd thrown them down and they'd landed behind the couch. Neither of them had remembered them in the morning, and now they lay on her carpet, drying quickly in the desert air.

"Throw them away, throw them away," her mind ordered crossly. She picked them up and walked all the way to the trash basket in her kitchen. But for some reason she couldn't throw them in. Instead, she took them to her room and laid them on her dresser. Then, as though she was moving in a trance, she went to get the other roses out of water. Cutting eight pieces of string, she hung each one upside down on her porch, just as she'd often done before to dry wild flowers she collected in the desert. She refused to think about why she wanted to save them. She refused even to look at them as they swung in the breeze. Walking away quickly, she forced her mind to go on to something else.

She went through the next morning like a sleep-walker, but she knew she would defeat herself that way and she managed to perk up toward noon. Eleanor was putting her through the last of her compulsory dives when Danni and her entourage entered the stadium.

Her eyes met Luke's across the blue water, held for just a fraction of a second, then his gaze slipped away as though they'd never connected at all. She turned and walked to the board, ready to block him out and continue with her diving.

It took all her mental strength to keep moving up the ladder to the board. She made her dive and swam to the side, ready to do it again. She would ignore him, erase him from her mind. She had to, even if he stayed all day.

But it seemed they were only coming through to say goodbye. Everyone on the swim team gathered around Danni, some even getting autographs. In the short time she'd been in Las Vegas she'd become quite a celebrity.

She waved to Jean and called, "See you at the games," then she was leaving.

Jean did a forward somersault and went down as far as she could, taking her time about coming back up. When she broke the surface she couldn't keep from glancing toward the exit. They were all leaving the stadium, with Luke at the rear. And he was limping.

Her heart caught in her throat and it was all she could do to keep herself from vaulting out of the pool and running after him. She jacknifed and dove down again, swimming as far as she could underwater. When she finally came up for air she was gasping and it took her some time to regain her breath. But she'd made it through her own personal crisis.

Luke was gone. It was over. And she had a lot of work to do.

The days began to go by at a dizzying pace. Every moment of her time was filled with work and training and study and sessions with Andy in the university pool. The only time she allowed herself the luxury of thinking about Luke was at night in the few seconds between the time when her head hit the pillow and her eyes shut with an exhausted snap that signaled total oblivion for the next seven hours.

Whenever she had a moment free during the day, she was in the department library, searching out new methods and exercises in hydrotherapy to use for Andy.

The boy was a dream to work with. He could go on for hours if she let him, going through every exercise she could cook up. If he ever tired, all she had to do was dangle the carrot of "the sooner you get back the full use of your legs, the sooner you can ride again," before his nose and he was off and running.

She'd been half-afraid he might be avoiding using his legs because of some deep-seated anxieties that might need psychological analysis, but once she started working with him she knew her fears were groundless. It just plain hurt when he tried to walk. And like any normal human being, he wanted to avoid pain. So she had to teach him ways of doing that, but give his legs a workout at the same time, until the healing process was complete.

She pulled him around the pool with a rubber ring under his armpits, yelling, "Kick, kick, kick." She had him pick up small stones from the bottom with his toes. She had him float, sink, turn somersaults and swim like a dolphin. And finally the time came when she could put the rubber ring away and have him swim the crawl and the breaststroke without help.

"When you can walk three blocks from your home and back without pain," she promised him, "the end will be in sight."

Meanwhile she was training more intensely than ever. "Slow down," Eleanor would complain. "You're making me dizzy."

"You'll have to go faster," she would reply, sailing by to try another maneuver. "I'm on permanent full speed ahead."

There were times when she went through moments of

panic. She wasn't at all sure she could go through with this. In a way, she was trying to be all things to all people, and she knew she couldn't keep it up forever.

"Just until the games," she would tell herself, throwing her body back into the ceaseless round of activity.

There were times when she regretted not having asked for her medallion back from Luke. Those times were usually very late at night. It was then that the memories came too, wrapped in shadows, sliding in on moonbeams.

The world looked different at night. Form was purple and black, spaces were shimmering silver, and the things that drove her in the daylight were harder to call up as a defense against the siren song of love.

A shadow on the wall recalled the line of Luke's profile, a hint of blossom in the air reminded her of the roses, now dried and sitting on her dresser. She could close her eyes and imagine Luke coming in through her sliding glass door, walking toward her bed, his step quickened with urgency. He would see her shape beneath the sheet and watch her sleep for a moment before flinging back the covers and joining her, pressing his strong, hard body to hers, waking her with the force of his passion.

At first she fought these dreams, trying to strengthen her wall of protection. But gradually she began to realize that there was a better way. If she let the dream float in and take possession of her mind, she found she could relax and fall asleep with something very close to a feeling of peace. And so she gave in to Luke again.

Of course, there was Jeffrey's engagement party to get through. She didn't really want to go, but she had received a formal invitation in the mail and felt she could not refuse. It seemed so final, another cutting of old ties. At first she toyed with the idea of calling one of their mutual friends to go with, but in the end she went alone. It was a kind of penance, she decided. She owed it to Jeffrey.

The engagement gift was a problem. It had to be something funny. There just was no other way. It would be expected of her. She racked her brain trying to come up with the ultimate in clever presents, but the perfect thing just wouldn't come to her.

She threw out every physical therapy joke that came to mind. Somehow they all seemed too crass. What if Mindy didn't have a sense of humor? Jeffrey had said she laughed at all his jokes, but that didn't prove anything.

Finally she went to Pookie's Exotic Bird Store. She wanted a parrot who said "Best wishes for a wonderful life," or something equally appropriate. Instead, she walked out carrying a large green bird with only one tail feather who croaked "Have a happy," incessantly and tried to bite her earlobe whenever she let her guard down. It was the closest she could come.

She felt like a fool carrying the animal into the restaurant where the party was being held. Everyone was dressed to kill and here she was holding a cage containing a nasty parrot.

"Have a happy," the bird screeched, glaring at Jean as though he were still planning strategy on her naked earlobe. She was careful to keep her fingers well away from the slate in his cage.

"God, how did you guess?" Jeffrey shouted the minute he laid eyes on the bird. "Do you know how long I've wanted one of these?"

Every person in the room turned to stare. The bird screamed "Have a happy," and Jean felt her cheeks flaming.

"Everyone should have one," she managed to get out before Jeffrey's laugh shook the room.

"Do you know how long these monsters live?" he asked at the top of his lungs. "Eighty, ninety years. Jean, this is what I call true vengeance. What did I ever do to you, anyway?"

It had been a stupid present and she wanted to sink through the floor. Jeffrey was laughing with real amusement but everyone else was laughing with disbelief. When the pretty dark-haired girl who was Mindy came up to join them, Jean wished she could run for home.

"It's Jean Archer, isn't it?" She held out her hand and Jean took the delicate little thing, feeling large and boorish. The girl was so small boned, her skin so clear and ivory she looked like a porcelain figurine.

"Hello, Mindy," Jean said in a rush. "I'm afraid I've brought a silly gift. You see, Jeffrey and I are always joking and...." *and so I've brought a practical joke to ruin your engagement party.* She couldn't quite say the words, but her mortified look must have implied them.

Mindy turned to look at the moth-eaten bird and Jean wanted to hide her eyes so she wouldn't have to see the pretty quiet face turn into a mask of justified rage. But she had to look. She deserved whatever she got and she knew it.

Mindy walked slowly toward where the cage was resting on the long linen-covered table. When she reached out to slide up the cage door, Jean took a step forward, wanting to grab her back and warn her about the sharp beak. But before she could do that, Mindy's arm was inside the cage and the bird was hoping onto her outstretched hand, tame as a woolly lamb.

"Thank you, Jean," Mindy said in her quiet voice. "This big fellow will go perfectly with my two cockatoos." She flashed Jean a full smile. "I love birds. I'm thinking of raising them as a full-time hobby."

Jean looked helplessly at Jeffrey and saw his proud

smirk. Suddenly they were all laughing and she knew
Jeffrey had made a wonderful choice. Mindy was a real
find.

The evening rolled by and she spent a lot of time
watching the engaged couple. They looked so happy together. Jeffrey was totally immersed in his career, yet he
had time for love. Why didn't she?

Luke, Luke, she whispered deep inside her soul. *If
only you wanted me the way I want you. If only I felt
strong enough to love you the way you deserve to be
loved. If only...if only....* What a fool she was! If she
wanted a championship, she went out and got it. She
wanted Luke. Why wasn't she working toward that
goal?

But her mind shied away from thoughts like that. She
was much too frightened to try anything so scary.

11

THE WORLD GAMES were only a week away when Andy didn't show up on time for his afternoon session in the pool. Jean paced the cement deck, fuming. She had no time for this. She had things to do. Where was that kid?

Bette usually drove him over, but now when they arrived fifteen minutes late, it wasn't from the parking-lot entrance, but from the door that led out onto the campus.

"You're late," Jean announced, noticing curiously that Andy's cheeks seemed red and his hair was damply sticking to his forehead.

"Yes, we are." Bette seemed a bit inane, grinning widely and watching Jean as though she expected some sort of reaction.

"Well," said Jean, perplexed, "what is it?"

"We walked," they said in happy unison. "All the way from home."

"Home" was a good ten blocks away.

Jean bit her lip and put her hands to her face. "And?" she urged. "Did you have any trouble? Is there any pain?"

"No!" Andy shouted, surging forward to throw his arms around her. "I'm going to be able to ride again!"

"Well, not quite yet," Jean laughed as she hugged him close. "But very, very soon."

There were tears in her eyes as she watched him walk

toward the edge of the pool and lower himself in. Tears
in her eyes and an exploding joy in her heart.

She'd thought winning the championship for the first
time was the greatest moment of her life, but there was
something so special in what she was feeling now, she
began to wonder if perhaps she'd been missing out after
all. Just seeing the smile on Bette's face, the glow in
Andy's young body, gave her a satisfaction she'd never
known before.

She continued to work with Andy right up to the day
before the World Games began. Eleanor was getting
very apprehensive toward the end.

"You'll never make it," she said despairingly, tearing
at her dark hair. "You just haven't trained enough.
You'll never make it."

"She'll never make it," the newspapers echoed, shaking their collective head and ruling Jean Archer out
of the games before they'd even begun. "She'll never
make it," the television sportscasters agreed. "There's
just so much fresh blood around she doesn't have a
chance."

It seemed the only one who believed she might even
progress past the preliminaries was Jean herself, and it
began to get awfully difficult keeping up her confidence
when everyone else thought she'd lost before she
started.

She thought she was composed and ready for anything, but when Eleanor said, "There was a big spread
on Danni Worth in this morning's paper. Did you see it?
She's back in town," her insides turned to quivering
Jell-O.

If Danni Worth was here, could Luke Chisholm be far
behind? Concentration crumbled at the thought.

But she hadn't worked this hard to let it all go in a
wave of emotion. As time went by and there was no

sign of Luke's presence in her city, Jean regained her equilibrium.

Las Vegas had always been a mecca for people from all over the world, but it had never seen such a flood of young people before. The gambling town took on the flavor of an international youth village, with bright eager faces from every land on every corner.

The university turned over its dormitories to house the athletes. The tree-lined walkways of the campus were crowded with muscular swimmers from Australia, dainty gymnasts from the Soviet Union, wrestlers from Argentina, fencers from Great Britain, sprinters from Norway, long-distance runners from Kenya—all meeting and blending in a giant sea of goodwill.

Jean wandered among them and she couldn't help but be buoyed by the feeling of comradery. Each entrant had a supply of tiny enamel pins depicting his own country's team and the sport he was entered in, and exchanges went on everywhere. By the time she'd finished one long walk on the first full day of the games, she'd collected pins from seven different countries and given out just as many of her own.

The opening day ceremonies were thrilling. She marched into the main stadium with the other entrants from the United States and felt a surge of pride in her country, and at the same time an overwhelming love for every other nation of the world, all together in the spirit of happy competition. This was the sort of thing she lived for.

And yet, as she walked along with all the other athletes, she found herself constantly scanning the crowd for the one face she dreaded seeing above all others. As if she could find Luke among the thousands and thousands in the stands.

Danni was there. She saw her and received a friendly wave in return for her smile. But she didn't see Luke.

The diving preliminaries began on the second day of the games. She went through the motions automatically, feeling like a robot.

"For heaven's sake," Eleanor scolded her, "get your head together. This is it, Jean. Time to come alive."

Danni was diving beautifully. Her body took off from the board like a bird in flight. Jean had to hold her breath as she watched. It was easy to see that Danni would become one of the greatest in the world very soon.

"Not yet," Jean whispered to herself. "It's still my turn."

Even though she herself wasn't diving up to par, she qualified easily. After her last dive of the day, she climbed from the pool and took the towel Eleanor handed her, wiped her face and then looked up straight into Luke's blue eyes.

Her heart seemed to stop in her throat. She stood frozen, not only by the shock of seeing him, but also by the glacial wall of ice in his eyes. Their gazes held for a long, long moment. Then he turned away and Jean watched as Sheila came up to take his arm.

They walked away, but Jean couldn't move. She'd known seeing him again was going to be painful, but she'd never dreamed it would hurt this much. She felt as though her world had been shattered by a crashing blow. She was paralyzed.

"Jean, come on." Eleanor obviously hadn't noticed what had happened to her. How could she expect her to move now? Now that nothing mattered anymore.

"Jean, let's go. I want you to do a double dose of flexibility exercises right away to keep you limber. You looked stiff out there."

Funny. It seemed her body would work after all. If

she told it very carefully what to do, where and when to move, her feet would take steps and her arms would pick up the towel and throw it into the wash bin. And here she'd thought her life was over.

As she followed Eleanor into the weight room, confidence began to flow back into her body. Yes, she'd faced the worst and she could still function. Maybe she would make it after all.

Still, it took her a good hour of meditation that evening to get herself firmly in hand for the next day's competition. She went to bed early and had a restful sleep. The next morning she went to the swimming stadium with her mind under control and a will to win as big as the Nevada sky.

She spent an hour swimming laps and warming up with some practice dives. Then she returned to the locker room and went to her mat for some last-minute meditation. A short time into it, a soft whisper interrupted her.

"Jean. Oh, Jean."

She smiled to herself, thinking how odd it was that people invariably felt if they spoke softly it wouldn't actually bother you. "What is it?" she asked the young swimmer who was trying to get her attention.

"There's a man outside who wants to talk to you."

Composure followed concentration out the window. "What's his name?" she asked, trying to tell herself she really wasn't shaking as badly as she knew she was.

"Luke somebody. He said to tell you he won't leave until you come out."

Jean rose slowly to her feet and pulled on a short robe before she went to the swinging doors that led out to the stadium. As she walked out, she seemed to be walking into the blue of his eyes, for that was all she saw.

"Hello, Jean."

She tried, but no words would come out. Hoping he wouldn't notice anything amiss, she nodded a bit desperately.

"I've got something for you." He held out her gold chain with the ace of diamonds medallion.

She stared at it, unable to utter a sound.

"I'm sorry I took it," he said, his voice gruff with what she realized with a start was agonized unease.

She looked up into his eyes and tried to read their emotion. "Why did you take it?" she managed. Suddenly she was very aware of the noisy crowd filling the stands all around the pools.

He shrugged his wide shoulders and turned to look at the water, his shoulder to her. "At first I told myself it was to give you a reason to get in touch with me again. But then I realized I'd taken it in anger."

"Anger?"

He turned to face her. "Anger. Jealousy. I wanted you to lose."

She reached out and took the chain from him, holding her hands close to her body so he wouldn't see the trembling. "Why?"

"Because you chose diving over me."

She closed her eyes. "It wasn't quite so cut and dried," she began, but he stopped her.

"Don't talk about it. Don't think about it. I wanted you to have your chain before the competition because I knew it was traditional with you."

She nodded slowly. "Don't you want me to lose anymore?"

"No." Suddenly he leaned down and kissed her quickly on the lips. "I want you to win." His smile was crooked. "Blow them away, water princess," he said unsteadily. Then he turned and walked back toward the crowded stands.

She stood where she was, watching him walk away. He was trying to hide his limp, but it was there. All she could think of was how angry she was with him for not getting it taken care of properly. She wanted to race after him and find out just what was wrong—whether he was in pain.

"Jean." Eleanor had come out of the locker room, looking for her. "What are you doing out here, counting the house? Get back in and get ready. We start in just a few minutes."

There was no time for more meditation to settle her down. Quickly she slipped the chain over her head. Confusion mixed with anxiety as she paced the cold floor of the locker room, trying to prepare herself for competition.

"Get hold of yourself, Jean," Eleanor barked at her. "This is no time to fall apart."

But Jean only heard her distantly, as though her voice was coming through a fog. As she walked out into the stadium with the other divers, she found herself searching the faces, looking for Luke.

Concentrate, concentrate, she told herself, but they were just words and she couldn't seem to get by that and really do it. Luke kept spilling into her mind, pushing aside everything else. She had to be called twice before she realized it was her turn to make the first of the required dives.

After a shaky start on her forward layout, the required dives went fairly well. She'd practiced each of them so often over the years she could practically have done them in her sleep, and as she got into the rhythm things began to fall into place.

She stopped looking into the crowd for Luke, but she felt his presence there every minute. When she badly missed her first optional dive, an inward somersault, she knew she was going to have to do something to wipe him from her mind if she was to finish even creditably.

She watched the others go through their paces, one by one. Danni was in fine form, and the Canadian girl was right behind her. In fact, everyone seemed to be peaking for this meet. There would be no slack to count on.

She did a creditable job on her next few dives, but with two left in the competition, she knew she was in trouble. She needed to nail her next dive in order to stay in the running.

Her reverse one-and-a-half with two-and-a-half twists was right on the money, and she earned a flock of nines from the judges, giving her a score of 63.

When Danni did her version of the same dive, Jean couldn't watch.

"What did she get?" she whispered to Eleanor, her back to the pool.

"She got 65," was Eleanor's terse reply. "You'll need at least a 67 on your last dive to have a chance."

Jean closed her eyes. A 67 was very near impossible. But it was absolutely mandatory. Keeping her eyes closed, Jean went into a short meditation, using the time to visualize the last dive she planned to make. Very carefully she watched herself as though she were on a television screen, watched every muscle, every movement that would go into making a perfect dive. Then she watched herself sail through the air, heard the applause of the crowd as she made the most magnificent dive of her life.

"Jean. You're up." Eleanor gave her a quick hug. "Good luck."

Armed with the picture she'd just projected, Jean mounted the board and prepared to do an inward one-and-a-half pike, which was her best dive. She stared straight ahead and quickly visualized the dive again, just as she'd done before. Her body should know it now. The pattern had been set. She stepped out onto the board and took off with a tremendous spring, cutting down through the air, then slicing into the water with a grace that tore through her body. She'd never done that dive so well before and she knew it.

Once again she couldn't look at the judges' cards. "What is it?" she hissed to Eleanor, once she'd sprung back out of the pool, dripping and shivering with anticipation.

"You got your 67."

In her great explosion of joy, Jean didn't notice that the score didn't seem to give the same satisfaction to her coach.

"Then, unless Danni pulls out a miracle, I've got it!"

But Eleanor was shaking her head. "I'm sorry, Jean," she said soberly. "I went over the figures again and I was wrong before. Even though you just made the best dive you've ever done, there is no way you can win this meet unless Danni's next score falls below 60."

A hard painful knot clutched at Jean's stomach. "Below 60? She hasn't had anything below 60 all afternoon."

Eleanor nodded. "Here goes the Canadian girl."

The Canadian girl, Grace Trevor, made a beautiful dive that assured her the number three spot. Then Danni stepped up. She was the last of the main contenders to dive.

Jean held her breath, her heart in her throat. Danni pranced out on the board, a magic elf dancing before an appreciative crowd. Then she was up and away, performing the multiple-somersault twist that was her specialty.

Suddenly something happened. In the flash of the de-

scent it was difficult for most people to see why she
landed wrong, but Jean saw it.

"She bent her head," she whispered, aghast. "That's a
beginner's mistake. She bent her head too much and lost
control."

The judges were charitable in the 59 they gave her.
The championship was Jean's!

"Danni!" Jean held out her hand to help the girl from
the pool.

"Congratulations old-timer," Danni grinned up at
her, then vaulted up to stand beside her. "If you'd been
coaching me, we could've had it together."

"Danni, I hate to take it this way. . . ."

"What are you talking about?" the girl cried, laughing. "So I goofed up my last dive. You goofed up your
first optional and landed a 55. That makes us even." She
grinned again. "Although some of us are more even
than others."

Jean shook her head. "I still feel guilty."

Danni groaned. "What should we do to assuage your
guilt? I know. Let's both hand over our medals to Grace
Trevor. Would that make you feel better?"

They laughed, hugging each other, and then Luke was
standing behind Danni and Jean began to back away.

"Hold it right there." Luke erased the distance between them in two giant strides and took her arm in his
firm hand. "Are you through here?"

She looked up at him mistily. "Through?" she asked
as though she'd never heard the word before.

"Through. As in finished. Completed. It's over."

"I. . .I'm finished with the diving if that's what you
mean."

He nodded coolly. "Good. You're coming with me."

"Luke!" She tried to pry his fingers from her arm. "Let
me go shower and then we'll talk. . . ."

He chuckled mirthlessly. "Oh, no you don't. I know you and your 'exit, exit, which one will she choose?' routine. You're coming with me right now."

She stared up at him, completely perplexed and not at all sure what he wanted her for. "I can't," she said, trying to pull away.

"You will." His hand on her arm underlined his statement. He had no intention of letting her go.

"Ladies and gentlemen," the crackling voice on the loudspeaker said. "The new and returning springboard champion is—Miss Jean Archer!"

People fell away from around her and, with a soft curse, Luke reluctantly let her go. She stepped forward to wave in appreciation of the wild cheering from the crowd. How wonderful it felt to be the favorite again and to have done it herself against all odds, against all advice.

She saw Eleanor standing with Mike at her side. She was smiling, her eyes bright with tears. And there was Bette in the front row, and Andy, both laughing with happiness over her triumph. With a sudden rush of joy she knew that what she shared with those people was as good as anything she could win with her diving. They were what life was all about.

The master of ceremonies brought the microphone in front of her so that she could say a few words to the audience.

"Thank you all so much for your love and support," she told them breathlessly. "I'd like to share this moment with Danni Worth and Grace Trevor who deserve it as much as I do." She motioned for them to join her. "And I'd also like to draw your attention to the marvelous performances of so many divers today. But for a quirk of fate or a missed step, any one of them could have been here in my place."

The audience cheered her again and she and her two cofinalists blew them kisses, smiling, waving, thrilling to the exulting music of appreciation.

"Medals will be awarded tonight at the banquet ceremony," the voice on the loudspeaker told the crowd. "There are still tickets available. . . ."

Danni and Grace left and Jean turned to go, but she ran smack into the solid wall of Luke's chest.

"Luke," she said quietly, aware of the live mike nearby, "let me go to the locker room—"

"Not on your life," he grated out, taking control with masculine precision.

"Wait," she said, trying to pull away and not noticing the expectant hush that had fallen over the crowd.

"I've waited long enough. You wanted to dive and I stood back while you rewon your championship." His eyes seemed to burn through her with blue fire. "Now it's my turn."

When he took her in his arms and kissed her with fierce ardor, she hoped the audience thought they were seeing a token of victory congratulation, but the surge of applause that came sweeping down from the stands gave evidence of the truth. They'd heard every word!

"Luke!" she gasped when he drew back again. "You're crazy!"

"No," he said, stopping to nod to the crowd as if he knew they were on his side, "I'm sane for the first time in my life."

Without warning he reached out and swung her up over his shoulder like a sack of flour, turned and began carrying her toward the parking lot.

"Luke," she whispered, "you can't do this!"

But the cheering from the stands drowned out her words and Luke had the gall to wave to the crowd before swooping her out through the exit. He carried her all the way to his car, while she cried out, kicked, made dire threats and giggled, all at once.

"I have never been so embarrassed in my life!" she announced as he settled her in his car.

"Really?" He slid into the driver's seat. "We'll have to work on that. I can think of lots of ways to embarrass you."

"Where are you taking me?" she demanded once they were moving along the street.

"To the Camelot," he answered calmly. "To my room."

"But what will people think?" she moaned, scrunching back into the corner. "I look like a Hallowe'en leftover."

They found out what people thought as heads turned on swivels throughout the lobby, and a crowd gathered to look her over while they waited for the elevator. Jean felt as though she were standing before the world, her naked body decorated with blue paint. To think she'd once been uneasy wearing simple clothes in this place. Right now, she'd be glad for any clothes at all.

"This is Jean Archer," Luke told those who gathered to gape. "She's just won the World Games springboard diving championship again, and now she needs to get a bit of rest."

Everyone nodded wisely as though they'd known it all along, but the two of them found themselves alone in the elevator, riding up.

"No one wanted to ride up with the weirdos," Jean giggled.

"In that case, we'll do this sort of thing all the time," he murmured, nuzzling her neck. "That way we'll always be alone and able to . . . ."

"Oh, no you don't." She pushed his hand away just in

time. The door purred open and they had a new little audience staring at them.

"This isn't the top floor," she remarked as they rushed along the corridor.

"No. I didn't take the King Arthur Suite this time," he admitted, putting his key into the door and opening up a simple double bedroom. "This is where I usually stay."

He ushered her in and closed the door behind them. "I've done a lot of thinking about our time together. I know I did everything wrong."

"You?" She whirled and walked nervously toward the sliding door that opened onto a small balcony. "I . . . I wasn't exactly a paragon of social graces."

"No," he agreed, coming up behind her and sliding his hands over her bare arms. "But then, it wasn't your place to be. I was the hunter. You were the prize."

"What?" She tried to turn to look him in the face, but his arms slid around her and held her still. "I don't know what you're talking about."

"I wanted you, Jean." He rubbed his rough cheek along the graceful curve of her neck. "I wanted you from the first time I saw you dive, so brave and strong and vulnerable."

Emotion choked her throat and she couldn't answer him, but he didn't seem to need a reply.

"I had to work hard to get you to come to me. I wasn't used to making that much effort, but I did it gladly, because I knew you were something so special, you had to be mine."

His hands slipped beneath the straps of her swimsuit, pulling them over her shoulders and down. "I brought you here and tried to dazzle you with jewels and fancy suites." He peeled back her suit until it hung at her waist, completely freeing her breasts. "I told you I wanted you in my life, and you thought it was for that—to go with the self-indulgent living. An affair to add to all the others. Didn't you?"

She had thought that, but that really hadn't been the reason she'd left that night. She turned, trying to tell him that, but his hands cupped her breasts, the rough palms teasing the nipples, and she gasped, her stomach dropping away.

"Jean, darling, that wasn't it at all." He let her turn and took her head in his hands, holding her face up to his. "I didn't want you for a fleeting diversion. I wanted you—I want you—for my own. For always. Even if I have to share you with diving. At least I'll have a part of you."

His mouth covered hers with sweet persuasion, opening the way to an ecstasy such as she had never known. "I love you, Jean," he whispered huskily into her mouth. "Please say you'll marry me."

"Luke...." She struggled to get enough room to talk. "That wasn't why I ran away. I thought you only wanted to talk me into being Danni's coach. Do you remember when we talked in the bar downstairs that last day? You were so happy when you thought I'd finally agreed to take the job. It broke my heart."

"Jean, Jean." He rocked her in his arms. "I was happy mainly because I thought it would keep you near me. I hadn't realized yet that I had to marry you. That there was no other way for me."

She looked into his blue eyes. "Why didn't you tell me?"

He shrugged. "I had to work this all out for myself, first, before I could explain it to you. And I wanted to leave you alone before the World Games. I didn't want to do anything more to destroy your concentration."

"I beat Danni," she said simply. "What will that do to your relationship with Sheila?"

He looked surprised. "You haven't ever thought there was anything between Sheila and I, have you? Sheila's engaged to marry a Texas oil millionaire right now. She and I have never been anything other than very close friends."

"Oh." She frowned. "But Danni was counting on the two of you getting together."

He shook his head. "Don't you worry about Danni. She's got more plans than the rest of us put together. She always bounces back and she's accepted her new father—well, not enthusiastically, but readily enough." He grimaced. "Of course, she's persuaded him to offer her skiing trips in Switzerland and her own small yacht in the process."

She laughed very softly and reached up to touch his dear face. "About diving—" she began, but he broke in.

"I watched you today and I know. You did a magnificent job, even after having me ruin things by coming up to you before the competition began. It's easy to see that you could go on another ten years if you wanted to."

She ducked her head. "If I wanted to," she repeated softly.

He put a finger under her chin to tilt her face back up. "What does that mean?" he asked intensely.

She smiled tremulously. "I'm retiring. I'm going to get into physical therapy full-time. I want to work with children like Bette's boy Andy."

He sighed happily, his arms tightening around her. "Child appreciation begins at home," he told her wisely. "Have you ever thought about having one of your own?"

She grinned at him. "Not until now."

His sure hands began removing the rest of her swimsuit. "It's something to think about."

Her fingers went to the buttons on his shirt. "I guess you're right," she agreed, opening the sides to reveal his muscular chest. "What do you think I should do about it?"

Her suit was down around her ankles and he leaned back to devour the sight of her naked body. "I'm going to show you," he promised smoothly, his hand tracing the line of her back down into the firm curve of her bottom. "But first I need a promise from you."

"Anything," she murmured, feeling deliciously lethargic. She began pulling the leather of his belt through the brass buckle. "Anything at all."

He tensed, holding back her hand as though this was too important to joke about. "Will you marry me?"

She met his gaze with sure confidence. "Do you love me?" she countered.

He took a deep breath. "I love you more than I've ever loved any other woman," he told her solemnly. "More than I ever will."

Her heart thrilled to his words. "Yes, I'll marry you, Luke, because I love you just that same way." She couldn't resist a small grin. "And because it's the only way I'll ever be sure someone is looking after your leg."

He laughed and took her to him before laying her across his bed. The love they made was full of joy and hope and even at the peak of their mad excitement, they could laugh and share.

"Are you going to miss diving?" Luke asked her later as they lay lazily side by side.

"Yes," she murmured sleepily. "Don't you miss football?"

He nodded.

"You know—" she raised on one elbow and looked into his crystal gaze "—no one ever knew exactly what it was about diving that I was clinging to. I don't know if I can really explain it to you."

"Try," he urged, brushing back her tousled hair.

She hesitated. "It was as though I could create something special out there on the board. I wanted so badly to have something of everlasting beauty."

He chuckled softly and pulled her to him again. "What you've got, woman," he told her gruffly, "is everlasting love. Will that do as a fair exchange?"

She smiled happily. "I guess I'll learn to cope," she admitted, wrapping her arms around him. "If I survive."

His laugh was deep in his throat. "That's what all that training has really been about all these years," he told her. "Didn't you know? It was to give you physical stamina." He nibbled at her ear. "Believe me, you're going to need it."

She giggled. "Everlasting love," she repeated. "I think I'm going to like that."

THE AUTHOR

A prolific author of romances, Helen Conrad
lives near Los Angeles, California with her
husband and four young sons. People often
ask her how someone raising a family has
time to think about romance. Her answer:
"Someone with four little boys *has* to think
about romance. Either that, or take up
skydiving. We all need an escape." Helen's
"escape" has brought reading pleasure
to many and will continue to do so.

COMING NEXT MONTH FROM
Harlequin Temptation ™.

BY MUTUAL CONSENT #5
Marion Smith Collins

When Toni Grey met fellow attorney Nick Trabert, she was smitten. Nick stirred her senses as no man ever had, but he was engaged to the one woman Toni would never dream of hurting....

THE FOREVER KIND #6
Alexandra Sellers

While on a solo "getaway" trip in the Canadian bush, actress Cady Hunter encountered devastating Luke Southam. They agreed to share a campsite that first night...a night that led to sharing far more.

CAST A GOLDEN SHADOW #7
Jackie Weger

Calico Jones trusted no man...until she rescued Irish McCaulley from a raging river. His tantalizing lovemaking brought her to the brink of ecstasy, but he soon wreaked havoc with her heart.

FOR NOW, FOR ALWAYS #8
Lynn Turner

Overwhelming passion had united the Hartmanns in marriage, but jealousy and misunderstanding had torn them apart. Eight years later, a penitent Neil returned to reclaim his wife. Proud Lacey said no, but her treacherously aroused body said otherwise....

FOUR TEMPTING
NEW TITLES EVERY MONTH